# The Best Animal Stories of Science Fiction and Fantasy

# The Best Animal Stories of Science Fiction and Fantasy

Edited by
Donald J. Sobol

FREDERICK WARNE

NEW YORK • LONDON

Frederick Warne & Co., Inc.
New York, New York

Text design by Meryl Sussman Levavi

Printed in the U. S. A. by the Maple Press Company

**Library of Congress Cataloging in Publication Data**
Main entry under title:

The best animal stories of science fiction and fantasy.

SUMMARY: Twelve eerie stories featuring animals, real and monstrous.
1.   Fantastic fiction, American.   2.   Fantastic fiction, English.   3.   Animals, Legends and   stories   of.   [1.   Horror   stories.   2.   Science   fiction.   3.   Animals—Fiction   4.   Short stories.]       I.       Sobol, Donald J.,       1924—
PZ5.B4196        [Fic]        79-5099
ISBN 0-7232-6169-5

Thanks are due to the following for permission to reprint the copyrighted material listed below:

"The Fog Horn," by Ray Bradbury. Copyright 1951 by Ray Bradbury. Reprinted by permission of Harold Matson Co., Inc.

"The Steel Cat," by John Collier. Reprinted by permission of A. D. Peters & Co. Ltd., London, England.

"The Monkey's Paw," by W. W. Jacobs. From *Selected Short Stories* by W. W. Jacobs published by The Bodley Head, London, England.

"The Large Ant," by Howard Fast. Reprinted by permission of the author.

"And, Lo!, the Bird," by Nelson Bond. Reprinted by permission of the author.

"The Smile of the Sphinx," by William F. Temple. Copyright 1950 by Hillman Periodicals Inc., for *Worlds Beyond*, December 1950. Reprinted by permission of the author.

"Dolphin's Way," by Gordon R. Dickson. Copyright 1964 by The Condé Nast Publications, Inc. Reprinted by permission of the author.

"Pithecanthropus Rejectus," by Manly Wade Wellman. Copyright by Street & Smith Publications, Inc. for *Astounding Stories*, January 1938 issue.

"The Exalted," by L. Sprague de Camp. Copyright 1940 by Street & Smith Publications, Inc. Copyright renewed 1968 by L. Sprague de Camp.

"Wolves Don't Cry," by Bruce Elliott; Reprinted by permission of the author and the author's agents, Scott Meredith Literary Agency, Inc., 845 Third Avenue, New York, New York 10022.

"The Chessplayers," by Charles L. Harness; Reprinted by permission of the author and the author's agents, Scott Meredith Literary Agency, Inc., 845 Third Avenue, New York, New York 10022.

"Mop-Up," by Arthur Porges; Reprinted by permission of the author and the author's agents, Scott Meredith Literary Agency, Inc., 845 Third Avenue, New York, New York 10022.

For
Barbara and Steve Davis

# Contents

## Other Books by Donald J. Sobol

Mr. Sobol is the author of the popular Encylopedia Brown series, as well as the following:

# The Fog Horn

## by Ray Bradbury

Out there in the cold water, far from land, we waited every night for the coming of the fog, and it came, and we oiled the brass machinery and lit the fog light up in the stone tower. Feeling like two birds in the gray sky, McDunn and I sent the light touching out, red, then white, then red again, to eye the lonely ships. And if they did not see our light, then there was always our Voice, the great deep cry of our Fog Horn shuddering through the rags of mist to startle the gulls away like decks of scattered cards and make the waves turn high and foam.

"It's a lonely life, but you're used to it now, aren't you?" asked McDunn.

"Yes," I said. "You're a good talker, thank the Lord."

"Well, it's your turn on land tomorrow," he said, smiling, "to dance the ladies and drink gin."

"What do you think, McDunn, when I leave you out here alone?"

1

"On the mysteries of the sea." McDunn lit his pipe. It was a quarter past seven of a cold November evening, the heat on, the light switching its tail in two hundred directions, the Fog Horn bumbling in the high throat of the tower. There wasn't a town for a hundred miles down the coast, just a road which came lonely through dead country to the sea, with few cars on it, a stretch of two miles of cold water out to our rock, and rare few ships.

"The mysteries of the sea," said McDunn thoughtfully. "You know, the ocean's the biggest damned snowflake ever. It rolls and swells a thousand shapes and colors, no two alike. Strange. One night, years ago, I was here alone, when all of the fish of the sea surfaced out there. Something made them swim in and lie in the bay, sort of trembling and staring up at the tower light going red, white, red, white, across them so I could see their funny eyes. I turned cold. They were like a big peacock's tail, moving out there until midnight. Then, without so much as a sound, they slipped away, the million of them was gone. I kind of think maybe, in some sort of way, they came all those miles to worship. Strange. But think how the tower must look to them, standing seventy feet above the water, the God-light flashing out from it, and the tower declaring itself with a monster voice. They never came back, those fish, but don't you think for a while they thought they were in the Presence?"

I shivered. I looked out at the long gray lawn of the sea stretching away into nothing and nowhere.

"Oh, the sea's full." McDunn puffed his pipe nervously, blinking. He had been nervous all day and hadn't said why. "For all our engines and so-called submarines, it'll be ten thousand centuries before we set foot on the real bottom of the sunken lands, in the fairy kingdoms there, and know *real* terror. Think of it, it's still the year 300,000 before Christ down under there. While we've paraded around with trumpets, lopping off each other's countries and heads, they have been living beneath the sea twelve miles deep and cold in a time as old as the beard of a comet."

"Yes, it's an old world."

"Come on. I got something special I been saving up to tell you."

We ascended the eighty steps, talking and taking our time. At the top, McDunn switched off the room lights so there'd be no reflection in the plate glass. The great eye of the light was humming, turning easily in its oiled socket. The Fog Horn was blowing steadily, once every fifteen seconds.

"Sounds like an animal, don't it?" McDunn nodded to himself. "A big lonely animal crying in the night. Sitting here on the edge of ten billion years calling out to the Deeps, I'm here, I'm here, I'm here. And the Deeps do answer, yes, they do. You been here now for three months, Johnny, so I better prepare you. About this time of year," he said, studying the murk and fog, "something comes to visit the lighthouse."

"The swarms of fish like you said?"

"No, this is something else. I've put off telling you because you might think I'm daft. But tonight's the latest I can put it off, for if my calendar's marked right from last year, tonight's the night it comes. I won't go into detail, you'll have to see it yourself. Just sit down there. If you want, tomorrow you can pack your duffel and take the motorboat in to land and get your car parked there at the dinghy pier on the cape and drive on back to some little inland town and keep your lights burning nights. I won't question or blame you. It's happened three years now, and this is the only time anyone's been here with me to verify it. You wait and watch."

Half an hour passed with only a few whispers between us. When we grew tired waiting, McDunn began describing some of his ideas to me. He had some theories about the Fog Horn itself.

"One day many years ago a man walked along and stood in the sound of the ocean on a cold sunless shore and said, 'We need a voice to call across the water, to warn ships; I'll make one. I'll make a voice like all of time and all of the fog that ever was; I'll make a voice that is like an empty bed beside you all night long, and like an empty house when you open the door, and like trees in autumn with no leaves. A sound like the birds flying south, crying, and a sound like November wind and the sea on the hard, cold shore. I'll make a sound that's so alone that no one can miss it, that whoever hears it will weep in their souls, and hearths will seem warmer, and being inside will seem better to all who hear it in the distant towns. I'll make a sound and an apparatus and they'll call it a Fog Horn and whoever hears it will know the sadness of eternity and the briefness of life.'"

The Fog Horn blew.

"I made up that story," said McDunn quietly, "to try to explain why this thing keeps coming back to the lighthouse every year. The Fog Horn calls it, I think, and it comes..."

"But—" I said.

"Sssst!" said McDunn. "There!" He nodded out to the Deeps.

Something was swimming toward the lighthouse tower.

It was a cold night, as I have said; the high tower was cold, the light coming and going, and the Fog Horn calling and calling through the raveling mist. You couldn't see far and you couldn't see plain, but there was the deep sea moving on its way about the night earth, flat and quiet, the color of gray mud, and here were the two of us alone in the high tower, and there, far out at first, was a ripple, followed by a wave, a rising, a bubble, a bit of froth. And then, from the surface of the cold sea came a head, a large head, dark-colored, with immense eyes, and then a neck. And then—not a body—but more neck and more! The head rose a full forty feet above the water on a slender and beautiful dark neck. Only then did the body, like a little island of black coral and shells and crayfish, drip up from the subterranean. There was a flicker of tail. In all, from head to tip of tail, I estimated the monster at ninety or a hundred feet.

I don't know what I said. I said something.

"Steady, boy, steady," whispered McDunn.

"It's impossible!" I said.

"No, Johnny, *we're* impossible. *It's* like it always was ten million years ago. *It* hasn't changed. It's *us* and the land that've changed, become impossible. *Us!*"

It swam slowly and with a great dark majesty out in the icy waters, far away. The fog came and went about it, momentarily erasing its shape. One of the monster eyes caught and held and flashed back our immense light, red, white, red, white, like a disk held high and sending a message in primeval code. It was as silent as the fog through which it swam.

"It's a dinosaur of some sort!" I crouched down, holding to the stair rail.

"Yes, one of the tribe."

"But they died out!"

"No, only hid away in the Deeps. Deep, deep down in the deepest Deeps. Isn't *that* a word now, Johnny, a real word, it says so much: the Deeps. There's all the coldness and darkness and deepness in a word like that."

"What'll we do?"

"Do? We got our job, we can't leave. Besides, we're safer here than in any boat trying to get to land. That thing's as big as a destroyer and almost as swift."

"But here, why does it come *here*?"

The next moment I had my answer.

The Fog Horn blew.

And the monster answered.

A cry came across a million years of water and mist. A cry so anguished and alone that it shuddered in my head and my body. The monster cried out at the tower. The Fog Horn blew. The monster opened its great toothed mouth and the sound that came from it was the sound of the Fog Horn itself. Lonely and vast and far away. The sound of isolation, a viewless sea, a cold night, apartness. That was the sound.

"Now," whispered McDunn, "do you know why it comes here?"

I nodded.

"All year long, Johnny, that poor monster there lying

far out, a thousand miles at sea, and twenty miles deep maybe, biding its time, perhaps it's a million years old, this one creature. Think of it, waiting a million years; could *you* wait that long? Maybe it's the last of its kind. I sort of think that's true. Anyway, here come men on land and build this lighthouse, five years ago. And set up their Fog Horn and sound it and sound it out toward the place where you bury yourself in sleep and sea memories of a world where there were thousands like yourself, but now you're alone, all alone in a world not made for you, a world where you have to hide.

"But the sound of the Fog Horn comes and goes, comes and goes, and you stir from the muddy bottom of the Deeps, and your eyes open like the lenses of two-foot cameras and you move, slow, slow, for you have the ocean sea on your shoulders, heavy. But the Fog Horn comes through a thousand miles of water, faint and familiar, and the furnace in your belly stokes up, and you begin to rise, slow, slow. You feed yourself on great slakes of cod and minnow, on rivers of jellyfish, and you rise slow through the autumn months, through September when the fogs started, through October with more fog and the horn still calling you on, and then, late in November, after pressurizing yourself day by day, a few feet higher every hour, you are near the surface and still alive. You've got to go slow; if you surfaced all at once you'd explode. So it takes you all of three months to surface, and then a number of days to swim through the cold waters to the lighthouse. And there you are, out there, in the night, Johnny, the biggest damn monster in creation. And here's the lighthouse calling to you, with a long neck like your neck sticking way up out of the water, and a body like your body, and, most important of all, a voice like your voice. Do you understand now, Johnny, do you understand?"

The Fog Horn blew.

The monster answered.

I saw it all, I knew it all—the million years of waiting alone, for someone to come back who never came back. The million years of isolation at the bottom of the sea, the insanity of time there, while the skies cleared of reptile-birds, the swamps dried on the continental lands, the sloths and saber-tooths had their day and sank in tar pits, and men ran like white ants upon the hills.

The Fog Horn blew.

"Last year," said McDunn, "that creature swam round and round, round and round, all night. Not coming too near, puzzled, I'd say. Afraid, maybe. And a bit angry after coming all this way. But the next day, unexpectedly, the fog lifted, the sun came out fresh, the sky was as blue as a painting. And the monster swam off away from the heat and the silence and didn't come back. I suppose it's been brooding on it for a year now, thinking it over from every which way."

The monster was only a hundred yards off now, it and the Fog Horn crying at each other. As the lights hit them, the monster's eyes were fire and ice, fire and ice.

"That's life for you," said McDunn. "Someone always waiting for someone who never comes home. Always someone loving some thing more than that thing loves them. And after a while you want to destroy whatever that thing is, so it can't hurt you no more."

The monster was rushing at the lighthouse.

The Fog Horn blew.

"Let's see what happens," said McDunn.

He switched the Fog Horn off.

The ensuing minute of silence was so intense that we could hear our hearts pounding in the glassed area of the tower, could hear the slow greased turn of the light.

The monster stopped and froze. Its great lantern eyes blinked. Its mouth gaped. It gave a sort of rumble, like a volcano. It twitched its head this way and that, as if to seek the sounds now dwindled off into the fog. It peered at the lighthouse. It rumbled again. Then its eyes caught fire. It reared up, threshed the water, and rushed at the tower, its eyes filled with angry torment.

"McDunn!" I cried. "Switch on the horn!"

McDunn fumbled with the switch. But even as he flicked it on, the monster was rearing up. I had a glimpse of its gigantic paws, fishskin glittering in webs between the finger-like projections, clawing at the tower. The huge eye on the right side of its anguished head glittered before me like a caldron into which I might drop, screaming. The tower shook. The Fog Horn cried; the monster cried. It seized the tower and gnashed at the glass, which shattered in upon us.

McDunn seized my arm. "Downstairs!"

The tower rocked, trembled, and started to give. The Fog Horn and the monster roared. We stumbled and half fell down the stairs. "Quick!"

We reached the bottom as the tower buckled down toward us. We ducked under the stairs into the small stone cellar. There were a thousand concussions as the rocks rained down; the Fog Horn stopped abruptly. The monster crashed upon the tower. The tower fell. We knelt together, McDunn and I, holding tight, while our world exploded.

Then it was over, and there was nothing but darkness and the wash of the sea on the raw stones.

That and the other sound.

"Listen," said McDunn quietly. "Listen."

We waited a moment. And then I began to hear it. First a great vacuumed sucking of air, and then the lament, the bewilderment, the loneliness of the great monster, folded over and upon us, above us, so that the sickening reek of its body filled the air, a stone's thickness away from our cellar. The monster gasped and cried. The tower was gone. The light was gone. The thing that had called to it across a million years was gone. And the monster was opening its mouth and sending out great sounds. The sounds of a Fog Horn, again and again. And ships far at sea, not finding the light, not seeing anything, but passing and hearing late that night, must've thought: There it is, the lonely sound, the Lonesome Bay horn. All's well, we've rounded the cape.

And so it went for the rest of that night.

The sun was hot and yellow the next afternoon when the rescuers came out to dig us from our stoned-under cellar.

"It fell apart, is all," said Mr. McDunn gravely. "We had a few bad knocks from the waves and it just crumbled." He pinched my arm.

There was nothing to see. The ocean was calm, the sky blue. The only thing was a great algaic stink from the green matter that covered the fallen tower stones and the shore rocks. Flies buzzed about. The ocean washed empty on the shore.

The next year they built a new lighthouse, but by that time I had a job in the little town and a wife and a good small warm house that glowed yellow on autumn nights, the doors locked, the chimney puffing smoke. As for McDunn, he was master of the new lighthouse, built to his own specifications, out of steel-reinforced concrete. "Just in case," he said.

The new lighthouse was ready in November. I drove down alone one evening late and parked my car and looked across the gray waters and listened to the new horn sounding, once, twice, three, four times a minute far out there, by itself.

The monster?

It never came back.

"It's gone away," said McDunn. "It's gone back to the Deeps. It's learned you can't love anything too much in this world. It's gone into the deepest Deeps to wait another million years. Ah, the poor thing! Waiting out there, and waiting out there, while man comes and goes on this pitiful little planet. Waiting and waiting."

I sat in my car, listening. I couldn't see the lighthouse or the light standing out in Lonesome Bay. I could only hear the Horn, the Horn, the Horn. It sounded like the monster calling.

I sat there wishing there was something I could say.

# The Steel Cat

## by John Collier

The Hotel Bixbee is as commercial a hotel as any in Chicago. The brass-rail surmounts the banisters; the cuspidor gleams dimly in the shade of the potted palm. The air in the corridors is very still, and appears to have been deodorized a few days ago. The rates are moderate.

Walter Davies' cab drew up outside the Bixbee. He was a man with a good deal of grey in his hair, and with a certain care-worn brightness on his face, such as is often to be seen on the faces of rural preachers, if they are poor enough and hopeful enough. Davies, however, was not a preacher.

The porter seized his suitcase, and would have taken the black box he held on his knees, but Davies nervously put out his hand. "No," he said. "Leave this one to me."

He entered the hotel carrying the box as if it were a baby. It was an oblong box, nearly two feet long, and perhaps a foot wide and a foot in depth. It was covered with a high-grade near-leather. It had a handle on the top side, but

11

Davies preferred to cradle it in his arms rather than to swing it by this handle.

As soon as he had checked in and was shown to his room, he set the box on the bureau and made straight for the telephone. He called Room Service. "This is Room 517," said he. "What sort of cheese have you?"

"Well, we got Camembert, Swiss, Tillamook . . ."

"Now, the Tillamook," said Davies. "Is that good and red-looking?"

"Guess so," said the man at the other end. "It's like it usually is."

"All right, send me up a portion."

"What bread with it? Roll? White? Rye?"

"No bread. Just the cheese by itself."

"Okay, it'll be right up."

In a minute or two a bell-hop entered, carrying a platter with the wedge of cheese on it. He was a black man of about the same age as Davies, and had a remarkable round face and a bullet head. "Is that right, sir? You wanted just a piece of cheese?"

"That's right," said Davies, who was undoing the clasps of his black box. "Put it right there on the table."

The bell-hop, waiting for him to sign the check, watched Davies fold down the front side of the box, which carried part of the top with it. Thus opened, it displayed an interior lined with black velvet, against which gleamed an odd-looking skeletal arrangement in chromium-plated metal. "Now look at that!" said the bell-hop, much intrigued. "Wouldn't be surprised if that ain't an *invention* you've got there."

"Interesting, eh?" said Davies. "Catches the eye?"

"Sure does," said the bell-hop. "There ain't nothing much more interesting than an invention." He peered reverently at the odd-looking apparatus in the box. "Now what sort of invention would you say that might be?"

"That," said Davies proudly, "is the Steel Cat."

"Steel Cat?" cried the bell-hop. "No kidding?"

He shook his head, a plain man baffled by the wonders

of science. "So that's the Steel Cat! Well now, what do you know?"

"Good name, you think?" asked Davies.

"Boy, that's a *title*!" replied the bell-hop. "Mister, how come I ain't never heard of this here Steel Cat?"

"That's the only one in the world," said Davies. "So far."

"I come from Ohio," said the bell-hop. "And I got folks in Ohio. And they're going to hear from me how I got to see this one and only Steel Cat."

"Glad you like it," said Davies. "Wait a minute. Fond of animals? I'll show you something."

As he spoke, he opened a small compartment that was built into one end of the box. Inside was a round nest of toilet tissues. Davies put his finger against his nest. "Come on, Georgie," he said. "Peep! Peep! Come on, Georgie!"

A small, ordinary mouse, fat as a butter-ball, thrust his quick head out of the nest, turned his berry-black eyes in all directions, and ran along Davies' finger, and up his sleeve to his collar, where he craned up to touch his nose to the lobe of Davies' ear.

"Well, sir!" cried the bell-hop in delight. "If that ain't a proper tame, friendly mouse you got there!"

"He knows me," said Davies. "In fact, this mouse knows pretty near everything."

"I betcha!" said the bell-hop with conviction.

"He's what you might call a demonstration mouse," said Davies. "He shows off the Steel Cat. See the idea? You hang the bait on this hook. Mr. Mouse marches up this strip in the middle. He reaches for the bait. His weight tips the beam, and he drops into this jar. Of course, I fill it with water."

"And that's his name—Georgie?" asked the bell-hop, his eyes still on the mouse.

"That's what I call him," said Davies.

"You know what?" said the bell-hop thoughtfully. "If I had that mouse, mister, I reckon I'd call him Simpson."

"D'you know how I came to meet up with this mouse?"

said Davies. "I was in Poughkeepsie—that's where I come from—and one night last winter I ran my bath, and somehow I sat on, reading the paper, and forgot all about it. And I felt something sort of urging me to go into the bathroom. So I went in, and there was the bath I'd forgotten all about. And there was Master Georgie in it, just about going down for the third time."

"Hey! Hey!" cried the bell-hop in urgent distress. "No third time for President Simpson!"

"Oh, no!" said Davies. "Life-guard to the rescue! I picked him out, dried him, and I put him in a box."

"Can you beat that?" cried the bell-hop. "Say, would it be all right for me to give him just a little bit of the cheese?"

"No. That's just demonstration cheese," said Davies. "Mice aren't so fond of cheese as most people think. He has his proper meal after the show. A balanced diet. Well, as I was saying, in a couple of days he was just as friendly as could be."

"Sure thing," said the bell-hop. "*He* knows who saved him."

"You know, a thing like that," said Davies, "it starts a fellow thinking. And what I thought of—I thought of the Steel Cat."

"You thought of that cat from seeing that mouse in that bath?" cried the bell-hop, overwhelmed by the processes of the scientific mind.

"I did," said Davies. "I owe it all to Georgie. Drew it up on paper. Borrowed some money. Got a blue-print made; then this model here. And now we're going around together, demonstrating, Cleveland, Akron, Toledo—everywhere. Now here."

"Just about sweeping the country," said the bell-hop. "That's a real good-luck mouse, that is. He certainly ought to be called Simpson."

"Well, I'll tell you," said Davies. "It needs one really big concern to give the others a lead. Otherwise, they hang back. That's why we're in Chicago. Do you know who's coming here this afternoon? Mr. Hartpick of Lee and Waldron. They don't only manufacture; they own the outlets.

Six hundred and fifty stores, all over the country! No middle-man, if you see what I mean. If they push it, oh, boy!"

"Oh, boy!" echoed the bell-hop with enthusiasm.

"He'll be here pretty soon," said Davies. "Three o'clock. By appointment. And Georgie'll show him the works."

"He don't never balk?" inquired the bell-hop. "He ain't afraid of being drownded?"

"Not Georgie," said Davies. "He trusts me."

"Ah, that's it!" said the bell-hop. "He trusts you."

"Of course I make the water luke-warm for him," said Davies. "All the same, it takes some character in a mouse to take the dip every time like that. Never mind—if he puts this deal over, we get him a little collar made."

"Mister," cried the bell-hop, "I want to see that mouse in that collar. You ought to get his photo taken. You could give it to anybody. They could send it back home to their families. Yes, sir, their folks 'ud sure be tickled to death to see a photo of that mouse in that collar."

"Maybe I will," said Davies, smiling.

"You do that thing, mister," said the bell-hop. "Well I got to be getting. Goodbye, Georgie!" He went out, but at once re-opened the door. "All the same," he said, "if I had that mouse I sure would call him Simpson."

Davies, left alone, set out his apparatus to advantage, washed, even shaved, and powdered his face with talcum. When he had nothing more to do, he took out his billfold, and laid six dollar bills one by one on the top of the bureau, counting them out as if he had hoped to find there were seven. He added thirty-five cents from one pocket, and a nickel from another. "We've got to put it over this time," said he to the mouse, who was watching him brightly from the top of the box. "Never get down-hearted, Georgie! That gang of short-sighted, narrow-minded, small-town buyers, they just don't mean a thing. This fellow's the guy that counts. And he's our last chance. So do your stuff well, pal, and we'll be on top of the world yet."

Suddenly the telephone rang. Davies snatched it up. "Mr. Hartpick to see you," said the desk-clerk.

"Send Mr. Hartpick up right away," said Davies.

He stowed away the money, put Georgie back in his nest, and dried his moist palms on his handkerchief. He remembered, just as the tap came on the door, to banish the anxious expression from his face and put on a genial smile.

Mr. Hartpick was a square and heavy man, with fingers twice as thick as ordinary fingers, and the lower joints of them were covered with wiry, reddish hair.

"Mr. Hartpick," said Davies. "I certainly appreciate your coming up here like this."

"Long as I'm not wasting my time," returned Mr. Hartpick. "Let's see the goods. I got a rough idea from your letter."

Davies had set the box on the table. Now getting behind it, he attempted a persuasive, hearty, salesmanlike tone. "Mr. Hartpick, you know the old adage about the better mouse-trap. You've been good enough to beat a path to my door, and . . ."

"Show me an idea, and I'll beat a path to it," said Mr. Hartpick. "However nutty it sounds."

". . . and here," said Davies, "is the Steel Cat." With that he flung open the box.

"Selling name!" said Hartpick. "Might be able to use the name, anyway."

"Mr. Hartpick, the idea is this," said Davies, beginning to count off his points on his fingers. "More mice caught. More humanely. No mutilation of mice as with inferior traps. No mess. No springs to catch the fingers. Some women are just scared to death of those springs. No family disagreements, Mr. Hartpick. That's an important angle. I've gone into the angle psychologically."

His visitor paused in the rooting out of a back tooth, and stared at Davies. "Eh?" said he.

"Psychologically," said Davies. "The feminine angle, the masculine angle. Now, the wife doesn't generally like to see a cat playing with a mouse."

"She can poison 'em," said Hartpick.

"That's what *she* says," said Davies. "That's the woman

angle. Poisoners throughout the ages. Lucrezia Borgia—lots of 'em. But a good many husbands are allergic to having their wives playing around with poison. I think a nation-wide poll would show most husbands prefer a cat. Remember, it was Nero—a man—fed the Christians to the lions. So that starts an argument. Besides, you've got to put a cat out, get it fed when on vacation."

"Any mice *we* catch, the missus flushes 'em down the toilet," said Mr. Hartpick with a shrug.

"Feminine angle again," said Davies. "Cleopatra fed her slaves to the crocodiles. Only many women haven't the level-headedness of Mrs. Hartpick to take a mouse out of a trap and get rid of it that way."

"Oh, I dunno," said Mr. Hartpick in tones of complete boredom.

"In one way this is the same sort of thing," said Davies, beginning to talk very fast. "Only more scientific and labor-saving. See—I fill the glass jar here with water, lukewarm water. It's glass in this demonstration model. In the selling product it'd be tin to keep the cost down to what I said in my letter. The frame needn't be chromium either. Well, having filled it, I place it right here in position. Kindly observe the simplicity. I take a morsel of ordinary cheese, and I bait the hook. If economy's the object, a piece of bread rubbed in bacon fat is equally effective. Now look! Please look, Mr. Hartpick! I'll show you what the mouse does. Come on, Georgie!"

"Live mouse, eh?" observed Hartpick, with a flicker of interest.

"*Mus domesticus*, the domestic mouse," said Davies. "Found in every home. Now watch him! He's found the way in. See him go along that strip in the middle! Right to the bait—see? His weight tilts the . . ."

"He's in!" cried Hartpick, his interest entirely regained.

"And the trap," said Davies triumphantly, "has automatically set itself for another mouse. In the morning you just remove the dead ones."

"Not bad!" said Hartpick. "Gosh—he's trying to swim! My friend, I think you may have something there."

"You know the old adage, Mr. Hartpick," said Davies, smiling. "It's the better mouse-trap!"

"Like hell it is!" said Hartpick. "Pure nut, that's what it is. But what I always say—there's a nut market for nut inventions. Play up the humane angle .... get the old dames het up . . ."

"Gee, that's great!" said Davies. "I was beginning to . . . Well, never mind! Excuse me! I'll just get him out."

"Wait a minute," said Hartpick, putting his heavy hand on Davies' wrist.

"I think he's getting a bit tired," said Davies.

"Now look," said Hartpick, still watching the mouse. "We've got our standard contract for notions of this sort. Standard rates of royalties. Ask your attorney if you like; he'll tell you the same thing."

"Oh, that'll be all right, I'm sure," said Davies. "Just let me . . ."

"Hold on! Hold on!" said Hartpick. "We're talking business, ain't we?"

"Why, sure," said Davies uneasily. "But he's getting tired. You see, he's a demonstration mouse."

Mr. Hartpick's hand seemed to grow heavier. "And what's this?" he demanded. "A demonstration—or what?"

"A demonstration? Yes," said Davies.

"Or are you trying to put something over on me?" said Hartpick. "How do I know he won't climb out? I was *going* to suggest you step around to the office in the morning, and we sign, if you're interested, that is."

"Of course, I'm interested," said Davies, actually trembling. "But . . ."

"Well, if you're interested," said Hartpick, "let him alone."

"But, my God, he's drowning!" cried Davies, tugging to free his wrist. Mr. Hartpick turned his massive face toward Davies for a moment, and Davies stopped tugging.

"The show," said Hartpick, "goes on. There you are! Look! Look! He's going!" His hand fell from Davies' arm. "Going! Going! Gone! Poor little bastard! Okay, Mr. Davies, let's say ten-thirty o'clock then, in the morning."

With that he strode out. Davies stood stock-still for a little, and then moved toward the Steel Cat. He put out his hand to take up the jar, but turned abruptly away and walked up and down the room. He had been doing this for some time when there came another tap on the door. Davies must have said "come in," though he wasn't aware of doing so. At all events the bell-hop entered, carrying a covered platter on a tray. "Excuse me," said he, smiling all over his face. "It's on the house, sir. Buttered corn-cob for Brother George Simpson!"

# The Monkey's Paw

## by W. W. Jacobs

Without, the night was cold and wet, but in the small parlor of Lakesnam Villa the blinds were drawn and the fire burned brightly. Father and son were at chess, the former, who possessed ideas about the game involving radical changes, putting his king into such sharp and unnecessary perils that it even provoked comment from the white-haired old lady knitting placidly by the fire.

"Hark at the wind," said Mr. White, who, having seen a fatal mistake after it was too late, was amiably desirous of preventing his son from seeing it.

"I'm listening," said the latter, grimly surveying the board as he stretched out his hand. "Check."

"I should hardly think that he'd come tonight," said his father, with his hand poised over the board.

"Mate," replied the son.

"That's the worst of living so far out," bawled Mr.

White, with sudden and unlooked-for violence; "of all the beastly, slushy, out-of-the-way places to live in, this is the worst. Pathway's a bog, and the road's a torrent. I don't know what people are thinking about. I suppose because only two houses on the road are let, they think it doesn't matter."

"Never mind, dear," said his wife soothingly; "perhaps you'll win the next one."

Mr. White looked up sharply, just in time to intercept a knowing glance between mother and son. The words died away on his lips, and he hid a guilty grin in his thin gray beard.

"There he is," said Herbert White, as the gate banged too loudly and heavy footsteps came toward the door.

The old man rose with hospitable haste, and opening the door, was heard condoling with the new arrival. The new arrival also condoled with himself, so that Mrs. White said, "Tut, tut!" and coughed gently as her husband entered the room, followed by a tall burly man, beady of eye and rubicund of visage.

"Sergeant-Major Morris," he said, introducing him.

The sergeant-major shook hands, and taking the proffered seat by the fire, watched contentedly while his host got out whisky and tumblers and stood a small copper kettle on the fire.

At the third glass his eyes got brighter; and he began to talk, the little family circle regarding with eager interest this visitor from distant parts, as he squared his broad shoulders in the chair and spoke of strange scenes and doughty deeds, of wars and plagues and strange peoples.

"Twenty-one years of it," said Mr. White, nodding at his wife and son. "When he went away he was a slip of a youth in the warehouse. Now look at him."

"He don't look to have taken much harm," said Mrs. White politely.

"I'd like to go to India myself," said the old man, "just to look around a bit, you know."

"Better where you are," said the sergeant-major, shak-

ing his head. He put down the empty glass and, sighing softly, shook it again.

"I should like to see those old temples and fakirs and
jugglers," said the old man. "What was that you started telling me the other day about a monkey's paw or something,
Morris?"

"Nothing," said the soldier hastily. "Least ways, nothing worth hearing."

"Monkey's paw?" said Mrs. White curiously.

"Well, it's just a bit of what you might call magic, perhaps," said the sergeant-major off-handedly.

His three listeners leaned forward eagerly. The visitor
absent-mindedly put his empty glass to his lips and then set
it down again. His host filled it for him.

"To look at," said the sergeant-major, fumbling in his
pocket, "it's just an ordinary little paw, dried to a mummy."

He took something out of his pocket and proffered it.
Mrs. White drew back with a grimace, but her son, taking it,
examined it curiously.

"And what is there special about it?" inquired Mr.
White, as he took it from his son and, having examined it,
placed it upon the table.

"It had a spell put on it by an old fakir," said the sergeant-major, "a very holy man. He wanted to show that fate
ruled people's lives, and that those who interfered with it
did so to their sorrow. He put a spell on it so that three separate men could each have three wishes from it."

His manner was so impressive that his hearers were
conscious that their light laughter jarred somewhat.

"Well, why don't you have three, sir?" said Herbert
White cleverly.

The soldier regarded him in the way that middle age is
wont to regard presumptuous youth. "I have," he said quietly, and his blotchy face whitened.

"And did you really have the three wishes granted?"
asked Mrs. White.

"I did," said the sergeant-major, and his glass tapped
against his strong teeth.

"And has anybody else wished?" inquired the old lady.

"The first man had his three wishes, yes," was the reply. "I don't know what the first two were, but the third was for death. That's how I got the paw."

His tones were so grave that a hush fell upon the group.

"If you've had your three wishes, it's no good to you now, then, Morris," said the old man at last. "What do you keep it for?"

The soldier shook his head. "Fancy, I suppose," he said slowly. "I did have some idea of selling it, but I don't think I will. It has caused enough mischief already. Besides, people won't buy. They think it's a fairy tale, some of them, and those who do think anything of it want to try it first and pay me afterward."

"If you could have another three wishes," said the old man, eyeing him keenly, "would you have them?"

"I don't know," said the other. "I don't know."

He took the paw, and dangling it between his front finger and thumb, suddenly threw it upon the fire. White, with a slight cry, stooped down and snatched it off.

"Better let it burn," said the soldier solemnly.

"If you don't want it, Morris," said the old man, "give it to me."

"I won't," said his friend doggedly. "I threw it on the fire. If you keep it, don't blame me for what happens. Pitch it on the fire again, like a sensible man."

The other shook his head and examined his new possession closely. "How do you do it?" he inquired.

"Hold it up in your right hand and wish aloud," said the sergeant-major, "but I warn you of the consequences."

"Sounds like the *Arabian Nights*," said Mrs. White, as she rose and began to set the supper. "Don't you think you might wish for four pairs of hands for me?"

Her husband drew the talisman from his pocket and then all three burst into laughter as the sergeant-major, with a look of alarm on his face, caught him by the arm.

"If you must wish," he said gruffly, "wish for something sensible."

Mr. White dropped it back into his pocket, and placing

chairs, motioned his friend to the table. In the business of supper the talisman was partly forgotten, and afterward the three sat listening in an enthralled fashion to a second installment of the soldier's adventures in India.

"If the tale about the monkey paw is not more truthful than those he has been telling us," said Herbert, as the door closed behind their guest, just in time for him to catch the last train, "we shan't make much out of it."

"Did you give him anything for it, Father?" inquired Mrs. White, regarding her husband closely.

"A trifle," said he, coloring slightly. "He didn't want it, but I made him take it. And he pressed me again to throw it away."

"Likely," said Herbert, with pretended horror. "Why, we're going to be rich, and famous, and happy. Wish to be an emperor, Father, to begin with; then you can't be henpecked."

He darted round the table, pursued by the maligned Mrs. White armed with an antimacassar.

Mr. White took the paw from his pocket and eyed it dubiously. "I don't know what to wish for, and that's a fact," he said slowly. "It seems to me I've got all I want."

"If you only cleared the house, you'd be quite happy, wouldn't you?" said Herbert, with his hand on his shoulder. "Well, wish for two hundred pounds, then; that'll just do it."

His father, smiling shamefacedly at his own credulity, held up the talisman, as his son, with a solemn face somewhat marred by a wink at his mother, sat down at the piano and struck a few impressive chords.

"I wish for two hundred pounds," said the old man distinctly.

A fine crash from the piano greeted the words, interrupted by a shuddering cry from the old man. His wife and son ran toward him.

"It moved," he cried, with a glance of disgust at the object as it lay on the floor. "As I wished it twisted in my hands like a snake."

"Well, I don't see the money," said his son, as he picked

it up and placed it on the table, "and I bet I never shall."

"It must have been your fancy, Father," said his wife, regarding him anxiously.

He shook his head. "Never mind, though; there's no harm done, but it gave me a shock all the same."

They sat down by the fire again while the two men finished their pipes. Outside, the wind was higher than ever, and the old man stared nervously at the sound of a door banging upstairs. A silence unusual and depressing settled upon all three, which lasted until the old couple rose to retire for the night.

"I expect you'll find the cash tied up in a big bag in the middle of your bed," said Herbert, as he bade them good night, "and something horrible squatting up on top of the wardrobe watching you as you pocket your ill-gotten gains."

## II

In the brightness of the wintry sun next morning as it streamed over the breakfast table Herbert laughed at his fears. There was an air of prosaic wholesomeness about the room which it had lacked on the previous night, and the dirty, shriveled little paw was pitched on the sideboard with a carelessness which betokened no great belief in its virtues.

"I suppose all old soldiers are the same," said Mrs. White. "The idea of our listening to such nonsense! How could wishes be granted in these days? And if they could, how could two hundred pounds hurt you, Father?"

"Might drop on his head from the sky," said the frivolous Herbert.

"Morris said the things happened so naturally," said his father, "that you might if you so wished attribute it to coincidence."

"Well, don't break into the money before I come back," said Herbert, as he rose from the table. "I'm afraid it'll turn you into a mean, avaricious man, and we shall have to disown you."

His mother laughed, and following him to the door, watched him down the road, and returning to the breakfast table, was very happy at the expense of her husband's credulity. All of which did not prevent her from scurrying to the door at the postman's knock, nor prevent her from referring somewhat shortly to retired sergeant-majors of bibulous habits when she found that the post brought a tailor's bill.

"Herbert will have some more of his funny remarks, I expect, when he comes home," she said, as they sat at dinner.

"I dare say," said Mr. White, pouring himself out some beer; "but for all that, the thing moved in my hand; that I'll swear to."

"You thought it did," said the old lady soothingly.

"I say it did," replied the other. "There was no thought about it; I had just— What's the matter?"

His wife made no reply. She was watching the mysterious movements of a man outside, who, peering in an undecided fashion at the house, appeared to be trying to make up his mind to enter. In mental connection with the two hundred pounds, she noticed that the stranger was well dressed and wore a silk hat of glossy newness. Three times he paused at the gate, and then walked on again. The fourth time he stood with his hand upon it, and then with sudden resolution flung it open and walked up the path. Mrs. White at the same moment placed her hands behind her, and hurriedly unfastening the strings of her apron, put that useful article beneath the cushion of her chair.

She brought the stranger, who seemed ill at ease, into the room. He gazed furtively at Mrs. White, and listened in a preoccupied fashion as the old lady apologized for the appearance of the room, and her husband's coat, a garment which he usually reserved for the garden. She then waited as patiently as her sex would permit for him to broach his business, but he was at first strangely silent.

"I—was asked to call," he said at last, and stooped and picked a piece of cotton from his trousers. "I come from Maw and Meggins."

The old lady started. "Is anything the matter?" she asked breathlessly. "Has anything happened to Herbert? What is it? What is it?"

Her husband interposed. "There, there, Mother," he said hastily. "Sit down, and don't jump to conclusions. You've not brought bad news, I'm sure, sir," and he eyed the other wistfully.

"I'm sorry—" began the visitor.

"Is he hurt?" demanded the mother.

The visitor bowed in assent. "Badly hurt," he said quietly, "but he is not in any pain."

"Oh, thank God!" said the old woman, clasping her hands. "Thank God for that! Thank—"

She broke off suddenly as the sinister meaning of the assurance dawned upon her and she saw the awful confirmation of her fears in the other's averted face. She caught her breath, and turning to her slower-witted husband, laid her trembling old hand upon his. There was a long silence.

"He was caught in the machinery," said the visitor at length, in a low voice.

"Caught in the machinery," repeated Mr. White, in a dazed fashion, "yes."

He sat staring blankly out at the window, and taking his wife's hand between his own, pressed it as he had been wont to do in their old courting days nearly forty years before.

"He was the only one left to us," he said, turning gently to the visitor. "It is hard."

The other coughed, and rising, walked slowly to the window. "The firm wished me to convey their sincere sympathy with you in your great loss," he said, without looking round. "I beg that you will understand I am only their servant and merely obeying orders."

There was no reply; the old woman's face was white, her eyes staring, and her breath inaudible; on the husband's face was a look such as his friend the sergeant might have carried into his first action.

"I was to say that Maw and Meggins disclaim all responsibility," continued the other. "They admit no liability at all, but in consideration of your son's services they wish to present you with a certain sum as compensation."

Mr. White dropped his wife's hand, and rising to his feet, gazed with a look of horror at his visitor. His dry lips shaped the words, "How much?"

"Two hundred pounds," was the answer.

Unconscious of his wife's shriek, the old man smiled faintly, put out his hands like a sightless man, and dropped, a senseless heap, to the floor.

### III

In the huge new cemetery, some two miles distant, the old people buried their dead, and came back to a house steeped in shadow and silence. It was all over so quickly that at first they could hardly realize it, and remained in a state of expectation as though of something else to happen—something else which was to lighten this load, too heavy for old hearts to bear. But the days passed, and expectation gave place to resignation—the hopeless resignation of the old, sometimes miscalled apathy. Sometimes they hardly exchanged a word, for now they had nothing to talk about, and their days were long to weariness.

It was about a week after that that the old man, waking suddenly in the night, stretched out his hand and found himself alone. The room was in darkness, and the sound of subdued weeping came from the window. He raised himself in bed and listened.

"Come back," he said tenderly. "You will be cold."

"It is colder for my son," said the old woman, and wept afresh.

The sound of her sobs died away on his ears. The bed was warm, and his eyes heavy with sleep. He dozed fitfully, and then slept until a sudden wild cry from his wife awoke him with a start.

"The monkey's paw!" she cried wildly. "The monkey's paw!"

He started up in alarm. "Where? Where is it? What's the matter?"

She came stumbling across the room toward him. "I want it," she said quietly. "You've not destroyed it?"

"It's in the parlor, on the bracket," he replied, marveling. "Why?"

She cried and laughed together, and bending over, kissed his cheek.

"I only just thought of it," she said hysterically. "Why didn't I think of it before? Why didn't you think of it?"

"Think of what?" he questioned.

"The other two wishes," she replied rapidly. "We've only had one."

"Was not that enough?" he demanded fiercely.

"No," she cried triumphantly; "we'll have one more. Go down and get it quickly, and wish our boy alive again."

The man sat up in bed and flung the bedclothes from his quaking limbs. "Good God, you are mad!" he cried, aghast.

"Get it," she panted; "get it quickly, and wish— Oh, my boy, my boy!"

Her husband struck a match and lit the candle. "Get back to bed," he said unsteadily. "You don't know what you are saying."

"We had the first wish granted," said the old woman feverishly; "why not the second?"

"A coincidence," stammered the old man.

"Go and get it and wish," cried the old woman, and dragged him toward the door.

He went down in the darkness, and felt his way to the parlor, and then to the mantelpiece. The talisman was in its place, and a horrible fear that the unspoken wish might bring his mutilated son before him before he could escape from the room seized upon him, and he caught his breath as he found that he had lost the direction of the door. His brow cold with sweat, he felt his way round the table, and groped along the wall until he found himself in the small passage with the unwholesome thing in his hand.

Even his wife's face seemed changed as he entered the

room. It was white and expectant, and to his fears seemed to have an unnatural look upon it. He was afraid of her.

"Wish!" she cried, in a strong voice.

"It is foolish and wicked," he faltered.

"Wish!" repeated his wife.

He raised his hand. "I wish my son alive again."

The talisman fell to the floor, and he regarded it shudderingly. Then he sank trembling into a chair as the old woman, with burning eyes, walked to the window and raised the blind.

He sat until he was chilled with the cold, glancing occasionally at the figure of the old woman peering through the window. The candle end, which had burnt below the rim of the china candlestick, was throwing pulsating shadows on the ceiling and walls, until, with a flicker larger than the rest, it expired. The old man, with an unspeakable sense of relief at the failure of the talisman, crept back to his bed, and a minute or two afterward the old woman came silently and apathetically beside him.

Neither spoke, but both lay silently listening to the ticking of the clock. A stair creaked, and a squeaky mouse scurried noisily through the wall. The darkness was oppressive, and after lying for some time screwing up his courage, the husband took the box of matches, and striking one, went downstairs for a candle.

At the foot of the stairs the match went out, and he paused to strike another, and at the same moment a knock, so quiet and stealthy as to be scarcely audible, sounded on the front door.

The matches fell from his hand. He stood motionless, his breath suspended until the knock was repeated. Then he turned and fled swiftly back to his room, and closed the door behind him. A third knock sounded through the house.

"*What's that?*" cried the old woman, starting up.

"A rat," said the old man, in shaking tones—"a rat. It passed me on the stairs."

His wife sat up in bed listening. A loud knock resounded through the house.

"It's Herbert!" she screamed. "It's Herbert!"

She ran to the door, but her husband was before her and catching her by the arm, held her tightly.

"What are you going to do?" he whispered hoarsely.

"It's my boy; it's Herbert!" she cried, struggling mechanically. "I forgot it was two miles away. What are you holding me for? Let go. I must open the door."

"For God's sake don't let it in," cried the old man, trembling.

"You're afraid of your own son," she cried, struggling. "Let me go. I'm coming, Herbert; I'm coming."

There was another knock, and another. The old woman with a sudden wrench broke free and ran from the room. Her husband followed to the landing, and called after her appealingly as she hurried downstairs. He heard the chain rattle back and the bottom bolt drawn slowly and stiffly from the socket. Then the old woman's voice, strained and panting.

"The bolt," she cried loudly. "Come down. I can't reach it."

But her husband was on his hands and knees groping wildly on the floor in search of the paw. If he could only find it before the thing outside got in. A perfect fusillade of knocks reverberated through the house, and he heard the scraping of a chair as his wife put it down in the passage against the door. He heard the creaking of the bolt as it came slowly back, and at the same moment he found the monkey's paw, and frantically breathed his third and last wish.

The knocking ceased suddenly, although the echoes of it were still in the house. He heard the chair drawn back and the door opened. A cold wind rushed up the staircase, and a long loud wail of disappointment and misery from his wife gave him courage to run down to her side, and then to the gate beyond. The street lamp flickering opposite shone on a quiet and deserted road.

# The Large Ant

## By Howard Fast

There have been all kinds of notions and guesses as to how it would end. One held that sooner or later there would be too many people; another that we would do each other in, and the atom bomb made that a very good likelihood. All sorts of notions, except the simple fact that we were what we were. We could find a way to feed any number of people and perhaps even a way to avoid wiping each other out with the bomb; those things we are very good at, but we have never been any good at changing ourselves or the way we behave.

I know. I am not a bad man or a cruel man; quite to the contrary, I am an ordinary, humane person, and I love my wife and my children and I get along with my neighbors. I am like a great many other men, and I do the things they would do and just as thoughtlessly. There it is in a nutshell.

I am also a writer, and I told Lieberman, the curator, and Fitzgerald, the government man, that I would like to write down the story. They shrugged their shoulders. "Go

ahead," they said, "because it won't make one bit of difference."

"You don't think it would alarm people?"

"How can it alarm anyone when nobody will believe
it?"

"If I could have a photograph or two."

"Oh, no," they said then. "No photographs."

"What kind of sense does that make?" I asked them.
"You are willing to let me write the story—why not the
photographs so that people could believe me?"

"They still won't believe you. They will just say you
faked the photographs, but no one will believe you. It will
make for more confusion, and if we have a chance of getting
out of this, confusion won't help."

"What will help?"

They weren't ready to say that, because they didn't
know. So here is what happened to me, in a very straightfor-
ward and ordinary manner.

Every summer, sometime in August, four good friends
of mine and I go for a week's fishing on the St. Regis chain
of lakes in the Adirondacks. We rent the same shack each
summer; we drift around in canoes, and sometimes we catch
a few bass. The fishing isn't very good, but we play cards
well together, and we cook out and generally relax. This
summer past, I had some things to do that couldn't be put
off. I arrived three days late, and the weather was so warm
and even and beguiling that I decided to stay on by myself
for a day or two after the others left. There was a small flat
lawn in front of the shack, and I made up my mind to spend
at least three or four hours at short putts. That was how I
happened to have the putting iron next to my bed.

The first day I was alone, I opened a can of beans and a
can of beer for my supper. Then I lay down in my bed with
*Life on the Mississippi*, a pack of cigarettes, and an eight-ounce
chocolate bar. There was nothing I had to do, no telephone,
no demands and no newspapers. At that moment, I was
about as contented as any man can be in these nervous
times.

It was still light outside, and enough light came in through the window above my head for me to read by. I was just reaching for a fresh cigarette, when I looked up and saw it on the foot of my bed. The edge of my hand was touching the golf club, and with a single motion I swept the club over and down, struck it a savage and accurate blow, and killed it. That was what I referred to before. Whatever kind of a man I am, I react as a man does. I think that any man, black, white or yellow, in China, Africa or Russia, would have done the same thing.

First I found that I was sweating all over, and then I knew I was going to be sick. I went outside to vomit, recalling that this hadn't happened to me since 1943, on my way to Europe on a tub of a Liberty Ship. Then I felt better and was able to go back into the shack and look at it. It was quite dead, but I had already made up my mind that I was not going to sleep alone in this shack.

I couldn't bear to touch it with my bare hands. With a piece of brown paper, I picked it up and dropped it into my fishing creel. That I put into the trunk case of my car, along with what luggage I carried. Then I closed the door of the shack, got into my car and drove back to New York. I stopped once along the road, just before I reached the Thruway, to nap in the car for a little over an hour. It was almost dawn when I reached the city, and I had shaved, had a hot bath and changed my clothes before my wife awoke.

During breakfast, I explained that I was never much of a hand at the solitary business, and since she knew that, and since driving alone all night was by no means an extraordinary procedure for me, she didn't press me with any questions. I had two eggs, coffee and a cigarette. Then I went into my study, lit another cigarette, and contemplated my fishing creel, which sat upon my desk.

My wife looked in, saw the creel, remarked that it had too ripe a smell, and asked me to remove it to the basement.

"I'm going to dress," she said. The kids were still at camp. "I have a date with Ann for lunch—I had no idea you were coming back. Shall I break it?"

"No, please don't. I can find things to do that have to be done."

Then I sat and smoked some more, and finally I called the Museum, and asked who the curator of insects was. They told me his name was Bertram Lieberman, and I asked to talk to him. He had a pleasant voice. I told him that my name was Morgan, and that I was a writer, and he politely indicated that he had seen my name and read something that I had written. That is normal procedure when a writer introduces himself to a thoughtful person.

I asked Lieberman if I could see him, and he said that he had a busy morning ahead of him. Could it be tomorrow?

"I am afraid it has to be now," I said firmly.

"Oh? Some information you require."

"No. I have a specimen for you."

"Oh?" The "oh" was a cultivated, neutral interval. It asked and answered and said nothing. You have to develop that particular "oh."

"Yes. I think you will be interested."

"An insect?" he asked mildly.

"I think so."

"Oh? Large?"

"Quite large," I told him.

"Eleven o'clock? Can you be here then? On the main floor, to the right, as you enter."

"I'll be there," I said.

"One thing—dead?"

"Yes, it's dead."

"Oh?" again. "I'll be happy to see you at eleven o'clock, Mr. Morgan."

My wife was dressed now. She opened the door to my study and said firmly, "Do get rid of that fishing creel. It smells."

"Yes, darling. I'll get rid of it."

"I should think you'd want to take a nap after driving all night."

"Funny, but I'm not sleepy," I said. "I think I'll drop around to the museum."

My wife said that was what she liked about me, that I never tired of places like museums, police courts and third-rate night clubs.

Anyway, aside from a racetrack, a museum is the most interesting and unexpected place in the world. It was unexpected to have two other men waiting for me, along with Mr. Lieberman, in his office. Lieberman was a skinny, sharp-faced man of about sixty. The government man, Fitzgerald, was small, dark-eyed, and wore gold-rimmed glasses. He was very alert, but he never told me what part of the government he represented. He just said "we," and it meant the government. Hopper, the third man, was comfortable-looking, pudgy, and genial. He was a United States senator with an interest in entomology, although before this morning I would have taken better than even money that such a thing not only wasn't, but could not be.

The room was large and square and plainly furnished, with shelves and cupboards on all walls.

We shook hands, and then Lieberman asked me, nodding at the creel, "Is that it?"

"That's it."

"May I?"

"Go ahead," I told him. "It's nothing that I want to stuff for the parlor. I'm making you a gift of it."

"Thank you, Mr. Morgan," he said, and then he opened the creel and looked inside. Then he straightened up, and the other two men looked at him inquiringly.

He nodded. "Yes."

The senator closed his eyes for a long moment. Fitzgerald took off his glasses and wiped them industriously. Lieberman spread a piece of plastic on his desk, and then lifted the thing out of my creel and laid it on the plastic. The two men didn't move. They just sat where they were and looked at it.

"What do you think it is, Mr. Morgan?" Lieberman asked me.

"I thought that was your department."

"Yes, of course. I only wanted your impression."

"An ant. That's my impression. It's the first time I saw an ant fourteen, fifteen inches long. I hope it's the last."

"An understandable wish," Lieberman nodded.

Fitzgerald said to me, "May I ask how you killed it, Mr. Morgan?"

"With an iron. A golf club, I mean. I was doing a little fishing with some friends up at St. Regis in the Adirondacks, and I brought the iron for my short shots. They're the worst part of my game, and when my friends left, I intended to stay on at our shack and do four or five hours of short putts. You see—"

"There's no need to explain," Hopper smiled, a trace of sadness on his face. "Some of our very best golfers have the same trouble."

"I was lying in bed, reading, and I saw it at the foot of my bed. I had the club—"

"I understand," Fitzgerald nodded.

"You avoid looking at it," Hopper said.

"It turns my stomach."

"Yes—yes, I suppose so."

Lieberman said, "Would you mind telling us why you killed it, Mr. Morgan?"

"Why?"

"Yes—why?"

"I don't understand you," I said. "I don't know what you're driving at."

"Sit down, please, Mr. Morgan," Hopper nodded. "Try to relax. I'm sure this has been very trying."

"I still haven't slept. I want a chance to dream before I say how trying."

"We are not trying to upset you, Mr. Morgan," Lieberman said. "We do feel, however, that certain aspects of this are very important. That is why I am asking you why you killed it. You must have had a reason. Did it seem about to attack you?"

"No."

"Or make any sudden motion towards you?"

"No. It was just there."

"Then why?"

"This is to no purpose," Fitzgerald put in. "We know why he killed it."

"Do you?"

"The answer is very simple, Mr. Morgan. You killed it because you are a human being."

"Oh?"

"Yes. Do you understand?"

"No, I don't."

"Then why did you kill it?" Hopper put in.

"I was scared to death. I still am, to tell the truth."

Lieberman said, "You are an intelligent man, Mr. Morgan. Let me show you something." He then opened the doors of one of the wall cupboards, and there were eight jars of formaldehyde and in each jar a specimen like mine—and in each case mutilated by the violence of its death. I said nothing. I just stared.

Lieberman closed the cupboard doors. "All in five days," he shrugged.

"A new race of ants," I whispered stupidly.

"No. They're not ants. Come here!" He motioned me to the desk and the other two joined me. Lieberman took a set of dissecting instruments out of his drawer, used one to turn the thing over and then pointed to the underpart of what would be the thorax in an insect.

"That looks like part of him, doesn't it, Mr. Morgan?"

"Yes, it does."

Using two of the tools, he found a fissure and pried the bottom apart. It came open like the belly of a bomber; it was a pocket, a pouch, a receptacle that the thing wore, and in it were four beautiful little tools or instruments or weapons, each about an inch and a half long. They were beautiful the way any object of functional purpose and loving creation is beautiful—the way the creature itself would have been beautiful, had it not been an insect and myself a man. Using tweezers, Lieberman took each instrument off the brackets that held it, offering each to me. And I took each one, felt it, examined it, and then put it down.

I had to look at the ant now, and I realized that I had not truly looked at it before. We don't look carefully at a thing that is horrible or repugnant to us. You can't look at anything through a screen of hatred. But now the hatred and the fear was dilute, and as I looked, I realized it was not an ant although like an ant. It was nothing that I had ever seen or dreamed of.

All three men were watching me, and suddenly I was on the defensive. "I didn't know! What do you expect when you see an insect that size?"

Lieberman nodded.

"What in the name of God is it?"

From his desk Lieberman produced a bottle and four small glasses. He poured and we drank it neat. I would not have expected him to keep good Scotch in his desk.

"We don't know," Hopper said. "We don't know what it is."

Lieberman pointed to the broken skull, from which a white substance oozed. "Brain material—a great deal of it."

"It could be a very intelligent creature," Hopper nodded.

Lieberman said, "It is an insect in developmental structure. We know very little about intelligence in our insects. It's not the same as what we call intelligence. It's a collective phenomenon—as if you were to think of the component parts of our bodies. Each part is alive, but the intelligence is a result of the whole. If that same pattern were to extend to creatures like this one—"

I broke the silence. They were content to stand there and stare at it.

"Suppose it were?"

"What?"

"The kind of collective intelligence you were talking about."

"Oh? Well, I couldn't say. It would be something beyond our wildest dreams. To us—well, what we are to an ordinary ant."

"I don't believe that," I said shortly, and Fitzgerald, the government man, told me quietly, "Neither do we. We guess."

"If it's that intelligent, why didn't it use one of those weapons on me?"

"Would that be a mark of intelligence?" Hopper asked mildly.

"Perhaps none of these are weapons," Lieberman said.

"Don't you know? Didn't the others carry instruments?"

"They did," Fitzgerald said shortly.

"Why? What were they?"

"We don't know," Lieberman said.

"But you can find out. We have scientists, engineers—good God, this is an age of fantastic instruments. Have them taken apart!"

"We have."

"Then what have you found out?"

"Nothing."

"Do you mean to tell me," I said, "that you can find out nothing about these instruments—what they are, how they work, what their purpose is?"

"Exactly," Hopper nodded. "Nothing, Mr. Morgan. They are meaningless to the finest engineers and technicians in the United States. You know the old story—suppose you gave a radio to Aristotle? What would he do with it? Where would he find power? And what would he receive with no one to send? It is not that these instruments are complex. They are actually very simple. We simply have no idea of what they can or should do."

"But there must be a weapon of some kind."

"Why?" Liberman demanded. "Look at yourself, Mr. Morgan—a cultured and intelligent man, yet you cannot conceive a mentality that does not include weapons as a prime necessity. Yet a weapon is an unusual thing, Mr. Morgan. An instrument of murder. We don't think that way, because the weapon has become the symbol of the world we inhabit. Is that civilized, Mr. Morgan? Or is the weapon and civilization in the ultimate sense incompatible? Can you imagine a mentality to which the concept of murder is impossible—or let me say absent. We see everything

through our own subjectivity. Why shouldn't some other—
this creature, for example—see the process of mentation out
of his subjectivity? So he approaches a creature of our
world—and he is slain. Why? What explanation? Tell me,
Mr. Morgan, what conceivable explanation could we offer a
wholly rational creature for this—" pointing to the thing on
his desk. "I am asking you the question most seriously.
What explanation?"

"An accident?" I muttered.

"And the eight jars in my cupboard? Eight accidents?"

"I think, Dr. Lieberman," Fitzgerald said, "that you can
go a little too far in that direction."

"Yes, you would think so. It's a part of your own background. Mine is as a scientist. As a scientist, I try to be rational when I can. The creation of a structure of good and evil,
or what we call morality and ethics, is a function of intelligence—and unquestionably the ultimate evil may be the destruction of conscious intelligence. That is why, so long ago,
we at least recognized the injunction, 'Thou shalt not kill!'
even if we never gave more than lip service to it. But to a
collective intelligence, such as this might be a part of, the
concept of murder would be monstrous beyond the power
of thought."

I sat down and lit a cigarette. My hands were trembling. Hopper apologized. "We have been rather rough with
you, Mr. Morgan. But over the past days, eight other people
have done just what you did. We are caught in the trap of
being what we are."

"But tell me—where do these things come from?"

"It almost doesn't matter where they come from," Hopper said hopelessly. "Perhaps from another planet—perhaps
from inside this one—or the moon or Mars. That doesn't
matter. Fitzgerald thinks they come from a smaller planet,
because their movements are apparently slow on earth. But
Dr. Lieberman thinks that they move slowly because they
have not discovered the need to move quickly. Meanwhile,
they have the problem of murder and what to do with it.

Heaven knows how many of them have died in other places—Africa, Asia, Europe."

"Then why don't you publicize this? Put a stop to it before it's too late!"

"We've thought of that," Fitzgerald nodded. "What then—panic, hysteria, charges that this is the result of the atom bomb? We can't change. We are what we are."

"They may go away," I said.

"Yes, they may," Lieberman nodded. "But if they are without the curse of murder, they may also be without the curse of fear. They may be social in the highest sense. What does society do with a murderer?"

"There are societies that put him to death—and there are other societies that recognize his sickness and lock him away, where he can kill no more," Hopper said. "Of course, when a whole world is on trial, that's another matter. We have atom bombs now and other things, and we are reaching out to the stars—"

"I'm inclined to think that they'll run," Fitzgerald put in. "They may just have that curse of fear, Doctor."

"They may," Lieberman admitted. "I hope so."

But the more I think of it the more it seems to me that fear and hatred are the two sides of the same coin. I keep trying to think back, to recreate the moment when I saw it standing at the foot of my bed in the fishing shack. I keep trying to drag out of my memory a clear picture of what it looked like, whether behind that chitinous face and the two gently waving antennae there was any evidence of fear and anger. But the clearer the memory becomes, the more I seem to recall a certain wonderful dignity and repose. Not fear and not anger.

And more and more, as I go about my work, I get the feeling of what Hopper called "a world on trial." I have no sense of anger myself. Like a criminal who can no longer live with himself, I am content to be judged.

# And, Lo!, the Bird

## by Nelson Bond

I don't know why I'm bothering to write this. It's undoubt-edly the most useless bit of writing I've ever done in a career devoted to defacing reams of clean copy paper with torrents of fatuous words. But I've got to do something to keep my mind occupied, and since I was in this from the beginning, I might as well set it down as I remember it.

Of course, my record of those first days makes no dif-ference now. But, then, nothing matters much now. Per-haps nothing ever really mattered much, actually. I don't know. I'm not very sure about anything any more. Except that this is an absurdly unimportant story for me to be writ-ing. And that somehow I must do it, nonetheless . . .

I've said I was in this from the beginning. That's a laugh. How long ago it really started is any man's guess. It depends on how you choose to measure time. Some four thousand years ago, if you're a fundamentalist adherent to Archbishop Usher's chronology. Perhaps three thousand million years ago, if you have that which until a few short weeks ago we used to speak of vaingloriously as "a scientific mind."

I don't know the truth of the matter, nor does anyone else, but so far as I'm concerned it started about a month ago. On the night our City Editor, Smitty, wigwagged me to his desk and grunted a query at me.

"Do you know anything about astronomy?" he asked a bit petulantly.

"Sure," I told him. "Mercury, Venus, Earth, Mars, Jupiter, Saturn, Uranus, Neptune, and something-or-other."

"How?" frowned Smitty.

"And Pluto," I remembered. "The solar family. The planets in the order of their distance from the sun. I had a semester of star-gazing at school. Some of it rubbed off."

"Good," said the C.E. "You've just won yourself an assignment. Do you know Dr. Abramson?"

"I know who he is. The big wheel on the university observatory staff."

"That's right. Well, go see him. He's got something big—*he* said," appended Smitty.

"Cab?" I asked hopefully.

"Bus."

"Astronomically speaking," I suggested, "a big story could mean a lot of things. A comet striking earth. The heat of the sun failing and letting us all freeze to death."

"Things are tough all over," shrugged Smitty. "The suburban buses run every twenty minutes until midnight."

"On the other hand," I mused, "he may have run into some meteorological disturbance that means atomic experiment. If the Reds are playing around with an H-bomb—"

"Okay, a cab," sighed Smitty. "Get going."

Abramson was a small, slim, sallow man with shadowed eyes. He shook my hand and motioned me into a chair across the yellow oak desk from him, adjusted a gooseneck lamp so it would shine in neither of our faces, then steepled lean white fingers. He said, "It was good of you to come so promptly, Mr.—"

"Flaherty," I told him.

"Well, Flaherty, it's like this. In our profession it isn't customary to release stories through the press. As a rule, we publish our observations in technical journals comprehensible, for the most part, only to specialists. But this time such treatment does not seem adequate. It might not be fast enough. I've seen something in the heavens—and I don't like it."

I made hen scratches on a fold of copy paper.

"This thing you saw? A new comet, maybe?"

"I'm not sure that I know," said Abramson, "and I'm even less sure I *want* to know. But whatever it is, it's unusual enough and, I suspect, important enough to warrant the step I'm taking. In order to get the swiftest possible confirmation of my observations, and of my fears, I feel I must use the public press to tell my message."

"All the news that's fit to print," I said, "and a lot that isn't; that's our stock in trade. What is it you've seen?"

He stared at me somberly for a long minute. Then:

"A bird," he said.

I glanced at him in swift surprise. "A bird?" I felt like smiling, but the look in his eyes did not encourage mirth.

"A bird," he repeated. "Far in the depths of space. The telescope was directed toward Pluto, farthermost planet of our solar system. A body almost four thousand millions of miles from Earth.

"And at that distance—" he spoke with a painful deliberation—"at that incredible distance, I saw a bird!"

Maybe he read the disbelief in my eyes. Anyway, he opened the top drawer of his desk, drew forth a sheaf of 8 $\times$ 10 glossies, and laid them before me.

"Here," he said, "See for yourself."

The first photograph meant little to me. It showed a field of star-emblazoned space—the typical sort of picture you find in any astronomy textbook. But on it one square was outlined in white pencil. The second photo was an enlargement of this square, showing in magnified detail the outlined area. The field was larger, brighter; a myriad of glowing stars diffused a silvery radiance over the entire plate. Against this nebulosity stood out in stark relief th firm, jet silhouette of a gigantic birdlike creature in fu flight.

I ventured an uncertain attempt at rationalization. said, "Interesting. But, Dr. Abramson, many dark spo have been photographed in space. The Coalsack, for in stance. And the black nebula in—"

"True," he acknowledged. "But if you will look at th next exposure?"

I turned to the third photograph, and for the first tim felt the breath of that thin, cold, helpless dread which in th weeks ahead was to come to dwell with me. It depicted a overlapping portion of that field surveyed in the secon print. But the dark, occulting silhouette had changed. Tha which was limned against the background of the stars wa still the outline of a bird—but the shape had changed. / wing which had been lifted now was dropped; the posture of neck and head and bill were subtlely but definitely al tered.

"This photograph," said Abramson in a dry, emotion less voice, "was taken five minutes after the first one. Disre garding the changed appearance of the—the image—anc considering only the object's relative position in space, as in dicated by the parallax, to have shifted its position to such an extent in so short a time indicates that the thing casting that image must have been traveling at a velocity of approxi mately one hundred thousand miles per minute."

"What!" I exclaimed. "But that's impossible. Nothing on earth can travel at such a speed."

"Nothing on *earth*," agreed Abramson. "But cosmic bodies can—and do. And for all that it has the semblance of a living creature, this thing—whatever it is—is a cosmic body.

"And that," he continued fretfully, "is why I asked you to come out here. That is the story I want you to write. That is why no moment must be wasted."

I said, "I can write the story, but it will never be be- lieved."

"Perhaps not—at first. Nevertheless, it must be released. The public may laugh if it chooses. Other observatories will check my discovery, verify my conclusions. And that is the important thing. No matter what it may lead to, what it means, we must learn the truth. The world has a right to know the threat confronting it."

"Threat? You think there is a threat?"

He nodded slowly, gravely.

"Yes, Flaherty. I know there is. There is a thing these pictures may not tell you, but that will be recognized instantly by any trained mathematician.

"That thing—bird, beast, machine, or whatever it may be—travels in a computable path. And the direction of its flight is—toward our sun!"

My interview threw Smitty for a loss. He read copy swiftly, scowled, studied the pix, and read the story again, this time more slowly and with furrows congealing on his forehead. Then he stalked over to my desk.

"Flaherty," he complained in a tone of outraged indignation, "what is all this? What the hell *is* it, I mean?"

"A story," I told him. "The story you sent me out to get. Abramson's story."

"I know that. But—a bird! What the hell kind of a story is that?"

I shrugged. "Frankly, I don't know. Dr. Abramson seemed to think it's important. Maybe," I suggested, "he's got rocks in his head?"

It was too subtle for Smitty. He smudged the bridge of his nose with a copy pencil and muttered something uncomplimentary to astronomers in general and Abramson in particular.

"I suppose we've got to print it," he decided. "But we don't have to make damned fools of ourselves. Lighten this up. If we must run it, we'll play it for laughs."

So that's what we did. We carried it on an inside page, complete with Abramson's pictures, as a special feature, gently humorous in tone. We didn't openly poke fun at Abramson, of course. He was, after all, the observatory chief of staff. But we soft-pedaled the science angle. I rewrote the yarn in the style we generally use for flying saucer reports and sea serpent stories.

Which was, of course, a terrific boner. But in all fairness to Smitty, how was *he* to know this was the story to end all stories? The biggest story of his or any newspaperman's career?

Think back to the first time you read about it, and be honest. Did you guess, then, that it was gospel truth?

We soon discovered our mistake. Reaction to the yarn was swift and startling. The *Banner* had been on the streets less than an hour when the phones began to ring.

That, in itself, was not unusual. Any out-of-the-ordinary story brings its quota of cranks crawling forth from the woodwork. Discount the confirmation of the local amateur observer who called in to verify Abramson's observation. His possibly lucid report was overshadowed by the equally sincere, but considerably less credible, reports of a dozen naked-eye "witnesses" who also averred to have seen a gigantic birdlike creature soaring across the heavens during the night. Half of these described the markings of the bird; one even claimed to have heard its mating call.

Two erstwhile civilian defense aircraft spotters called to identify the object variously, but with equal assurance, as a B-29 and a Russian superjet. A member of the Audubon Society identified the bird as a ruby-throated nuthatch which, he suggested, must have flown in front of the telescope just as the camera clicked. An itinerant preacher of an obscure cult marched into our office to inform us with savage delight that this was the veritable bird foretold in the book of Revelations, and that the end of the world could now be expected momentarily, if not sooner.

These were the lunatic fringe. What was unusual was that all the calls which flooded our office during the next twenty-four hours were not made by screwballs and fanatics. Some were of great importance, not only to their instigators but to the scientific world, and to mankind in general.

We had fed a take to the Associated Press. To our astonishment, from that syndicate we received an immediate demand for follow-up material, including copies of Abramson's pix. The national picture magazines were even more on their toes. They flew their own boys to town and had contacted Abramson for a second story before we wised up to the fact that we had broken the number-one sensation of the year.

Meanwhile, and most important of all, astronomers elsewhere throughout the world set their big eyes for the area of the thing first spotted by Dr. Abramson. And within twenty-four hours, to the stunned dismay of all who, like Smitty and myself, had seen it as a terrific joke, verifications were forthcoming from every observatory that enjoyed good viewing conditions. What's more, mathematicians verified Abramson's estimates as to the thing's speed and trajectory. The bird, estimated to be larger in size than any solar planet, was conceded to be somewhere in the vicinity of Pluto—and approaching our sun at a speed of 145,000,000 miles per day!

By the end of the first week, the bird was visible through any fair-sized telescope. The story snowballed, and in its rolling picked up all the oddments lying in its path. A character who introduced himself as a member of the Fortean Society—whatever that is—came to the office armed with a thick volume in which he pointed out to us a dozen paragraphs purporting to prove that similar dark objects had been seen in the skies above various parts of the world over a period of several hundred years.

The central council of the P.T.A. issued a plaintive statement deploring scare-journalism and its evil effects on the youth of our nation. The Daughters of the American Revolution passed a resolution branding the strange image a new secret weapon of the Kremlin's lads, and urging that immediate steps—undefined but drastic—be taken by the authorities. A special committee of the local ministers' association called to advise us that the story we had originated tended to undermine the religious faith of the community;

they demanded that we print a full retraction of the hoax in the earliest possible edition.

Which was, by this time, a complete impossibility. Before the end of the second week, the black dot in the skies could be viewed with binoculars. By the middle of the third week it had reached the stage of naked-eye visibility. Crowds gathered in the streets when this became known, and those with good eyesight professed to be able to discern the rhythmic rise and fall of those tremendous wings, now familiar to all because of the scores of photographs which by this time had appeared in every newspaper and magazine of any importance.

The cadenced beating of those monstrous wings was but one of the many inexplicable—or at least unexplained—mysteries about the creature from beyond. Vainly a few die-hard physicists pointed out that wings are of no propulsive help in airless void, that alate flight is possible only where there are wind currents to lift and carry. The thing flew. And whether its gigantic pinions beat, as some men thought, on an interstellar atmosphere unguessed by Earthly science, or whether they stroked against beams of light or quantum bundles, as others contended, these were meaningless quibbles in the face of that one, stark, incontrovertible fact: the thing flew.

With the dawning of the fourth week, the bird from outer space reached Jupiter and dwarfed it—an ominous black interloper equal in size to any cosmic neighbor man had ever seen.

I sat alone with Abramson in his office. Abramson was tired and, I think, a little ill. His smile was not a success, nor had his words their hoped-for jauntiness.

"Well, I got what I wanted, Flaherty," he admitted. "I wanted swift action, and got it. Though what good it is, I don't know. The world recognizes its danger now, and is helpless to do anything about it."

"It has hurdled the asteroids," I said. "Now it's approaching Mars, and is still moving sunward. Everyone is asking, though, why doesn't its presence within the system raise merry hob with celestial mechanics? By all known laws it should have thrown everything out of balance. A creature of that size, with its gravitational attraction—"

"You're still thinking in old terms, my boy. Now we are confronted with something strange and new. Who knows what laws may govern the Bird of Time?"

"The Bird of Time? I seem to have heard that phrase."

"Of course." He quoted moodily, "'The Bird of Time has but a little way to fly—and Lo!, the Bird is on the Wing.'"

"The *Rubaiyat*," I remembered.

"Yes. Omar was an astronomer, you know, as well as a poet. He must have known—or guessed—something of this." Abramson gestured wanly skyward. "Indeed, many of the ancients seem to have known something about it. I've been doing a lot of research during these past weeks, Flaherty. It is amazing how many references there are in the old writings to a great bird of space—statements which until recently did not seem to be at all significant or important, but which now hold a greater and graver meaning for us."

"Such as?"

"Culture myths," he said. "Legends. The records of a hundred vanished races. The Mayan myth of the space-swallow, the Toltec quetzlcoatl, the Russian firebird, the phoenix of the Greeks."

"We don't know yet," I argued, "that it *is* a bird."

He shrugged.

"A bird, a giant mammal, a pterodactyl, some similar creature on a cosmic scale—what does it matter? Perhaps it is a life-form foreign to anything we know, something we can only try to name in earthly terms, describe by earthly analogies. The ancients called it a bird. The Phoenicians worshipped the 'bird that was, and is again to be.' The Persians wrote of the fabulous roc. There is an Aramaic legend of the giant bird that rules—and spawns—the worlds."

"Spawns the worlds?"

"Why else should it be coming?" he inquired. "Does its

great size mean nothing to you?" He stared at me thoughtfully for a moment. Then: "Flaherty," he asked strangely, "what is the earth?"

"Why," I replied, "the world we live on. A planet."

"Yes. But what is a planet?"

"A unit of the solar system. A part of the sun's family."

"Do you *know* that? Or are you simply parroting things you were taught in school?"

"The latter, of course. But what else could it be?"

"Our earth could be," he answered reluctantly, "no part of the sun's family at all. Many theories have been devised, Flaherty, to explain earth's place in this tiny segment of the universe which we call the solar system. None of them are provably inaccurate. But on the other hand, none are demonstrably true.

"There is the nebular hypothesis: the theory that earth and its sister planets were born of a contracting sun. Were in fact, small globules of solar matter left to cool in orbits deserted by their condensing parent. A late refinement of this theory makes us the product of materials derived from a sister sun, once twin to our own orb.

"The planetesimal and tidal theories each are based on the assumption that unfathomable eons ago another sun by passed our own, and that the planets are the offspring of that ancient, flaming rendezvous in space.

"Each of these theories has its proponents and its opponents; each has its verifications and denials. None can be wholly proven or refuted.

"But—" he stirred restlessly "—there is another possibility which, to the best of my knowledge, has never been expanded. Yet it is equally valid to any I have mentioned. And in the light of that which we now know, it seems to me more likely than any other.

"It is that earth and its sister planets have nothing whatever to do with the sun. That they are not, nor ever were, mere members of its family. That the sun in our skies is simply a convenience."

"Convenience?" I frowned. "Convenience for what?"

"For the bird," said Abramson unhappily. "For the great bird which is our parent. Flaherty, can you conceive that our sun may be a cosmic incubator. And that the world on which we live may be merely—an egg?"

I stared at him. "An egg! Fantastic!"

"You think so? You can look at the pictures, read the stories in the magazines, see the approaching bird with your own eyes, and still think there exists anything more incredible than that which has befallen us?"

"But an egg! Eggs are egg-shaped. Ovoid."

"The eggs of some birds are ovoid. But those of the plover are pear-shaped, those of the sand-grous cylindrical, those of the grebe biconical. There are eggs shaped like spindles and spears. The eggs of owls, and of mammals, are generally spheroid. As is the earth."

"But eggs have shells!"

"As does our earth. Earth's crust is but forty miles thick—a layer for a body of its size comparable in every respect to the shell of an egg. Moreover, it is a smooth shell. Earth's greatest height is Mount Everest, some thirty thousand feet; its greatest depth is Swire Deep in the Pacific, thirty-five thousand. A maximum variation of about twelve miles. To feel these irregularities on a twelve-inch model of the earth you would need the delicate fingers of the blind, because the greatest height protrudes but the hundred and twentieth part of an inch, and the lowest depth is but one hundredth part of an inch below its surface."

"Still," I argued desperately, "you can't be right. You've overlooked the most important fact. Eggs hold life! Eggs contain the fledglings of the creature that spawned them. Eggs crack open and—"

I stopped abruptly. Abramson nodded, creaking back and forth in his ancient swivel chair, the creaking a monotonous rhythm to his nodding. There was sadness in his eyes and in his voice.

"Even so," he said wearily. "Even so . . ."

So that was the second great story which I broke. I was still fool enough to get a bang out of it at the time; I don't

feel the same way about it now. But, then, I don't feel th
same about anything any more. I guess you can understan
that. The coming of the bird was such a big thing, such
truly big thing, that it dwindled into insignificance all th
things we used to consider great, important, world-shaking

World-shaking!

I'll make it brief. There's so little purpose to my tellin
of this story. But there may be in it, here and there, a fac
you do not know. And I've got to do something—any
thing—to keep myself from thinking.

You remember that grim fourth week, and the stead
approach of the bird. We had settled for calling it that b
then. We were not sure if it were bird or winged beast, bu
men think—and give names to things—in terms of familia
objects. And that slim black shape with its tremendou
wings, its taloned legs and long, cruel, curving beak, looke
more like a bird than an animal.

Besides, there was Abramson's world-egg theory to b
considered. The people, hearing this, doubted it with a furi
ous hope—but feared it might be true. Men in high posi
tions asked what could be done. They sent for Abramson
and he advised them. He could be wrong, he acknowledged
But if he were right, there was only one hope for salvation
The life within Earth must be stilled.

"I believe," he told a special emergency committee
appointed by the President, "the bird has come to hatch the
brood of young it deposited God knows how many centur
ies ago about that incubating warmth which is our sun. Its
wisdom or its instinct tells it that the time of emergence is
now; it has come to help its fledglings shed their shells.

"But we know that mother birds, alone and unaided, do
not hatch their young. They will aid a struggling chick to
crack its shell, but they will never begin the liberating ac
tion. With an uncanny second sense, they seem to know
which eggs have failed to develop life within them. Such
eggs they never disturb.

"Therein, gentlemen, lies our only hope. The shell of

Earth is forty miles in thickness. We have our engineers and technicians; we have the atomic bomb. If mankind is to live, the host to which we are but parasites must die. That is my only solution. I leave the rest to you."

He left them, still wrangling, in Washington, and returned home. He saw little hope, he told me the next day, of their reaching any firm decision in sufficient time to act. Abramson, I think, had already resigned himself to the inevitable, had with a wan grimace surrendered mankind to its fate. He said once that bureaucracy had achieved its ultimate destiny. It had throttled itself to death with its own red tape.

And still the bird moved sunward. On the twenty-eighth day it made its nearest approach to Earth, and passed us by. I don't know—nor can the scientist explain—why our globe was not shattered by the gravitational attraction of that gigantic mass. Perhaps because the Newtonian theory is, after all, simply a theory, and has no actuality in fact. I don't know. If there were time it would be good to resurvey the facts and learn the truth about such things. At any rate, all things considered, we suffered very little from its nearness. There were high tides and mighty winds; those sections of earth subject to earthquakes suffered some mild tremors. But that is all.

Then we won a respite. You remember how the bird paused in its headlong flight to hover for two full days about that tiniest of the solar planets—the one we call Mercury. Briefly, as if searching for something, it flew in a wide circle in an orbit between Mercury and the sun.

Abramson believed it *was* looking for something. For something it could not find because it was no longer there. Astronomers believed, said Abramson, that at one time there had been another planet circling between Mercury and the sun. Some watchers of the sky had seen this as late as the Eighteenth Century, and had called it Vulcan. Vulcan had disappeared; perhaps had fallen into the sun. So thought Abramson. And so, apparently, the bird decided, too, for

after a fruitless search it winged its way outward from the
sun to approach the closest of its brood still remaining in-
tact.

Must I remind you of that dreadful day? I think not. No
man alive will ever forget what he saw then. The bird approaching Mercury, pausing to hover motionless above a
planet which seemed a mote beneath the umbra of those
massive wings. Men in the streets saw this. I saw more, for I
stood beside Abramson in the university observatory,
watching that scene with the aid of a telescope.

I saw the first thin splitting of Mercury's shell, and the
curious fluid ichor which seeped from a dying world. I
watched the grisly emergence of that small, wet, scrawny
thing—raw simulacrum of its monstrous parent—from the
egg in which it had lain for whatever incalculable era was
the gestation period of a creature vast as space and old as
time. I saw the mother bird stretch forth its giant beak and
help its fledgling rid itself of a peeling, needless shell; stood
horrified to watch the younger bird emerge and flap its
new, uncertain wings, drying them in the burning rays of
the star which had been its incubator.

And I saw the shredded remnants of a world spiral into
the sun which was its pyre.

It was then, at last, that mankind woke to action. The
doubters were finally convinced, those who had argued
against the "needless expense" and folly of Abramson's plan
were silenced. Forgotten now were selfishness and greed,
political differences and departmental strife. The world it
infested trembled on the brink of doom—and a race of vermin battled for its life.

In the flat desertland of America was frantically
thrown together the mechanism for mankind's greatest pro-
ject—Operation Life. To this desert flew the miners, the
construction engineers, the nuclear physicists, the men
skilled in deep-drilling operations. There they began their
task, working night and day with a speed which heretofore
had been called impossible. There they are working now,
this minute, as I write, fighting desperately against each

passing second of time, striving with every means and method they know to reach and destroy, before the bird comes, the life within our world.

A week ago the bird moved on to Venus. Throughout these seven days we have watched its progress there. We cannot see much through the eternal veil of mist which surrounds our sister planet, so we do not know what has for so gratefully long a time occupied the bird. Whatever it is, we are thankful for it. We wait and watch. And as we watch, we work. And as we work, we pray. . . .

So there is no real ending to this story. As I said before, I don't know why I'm bothering to write it. The answer is not ready to be given. If we succeed, there will be ample time to tell the tale properly—the whole great story, fully documented, of the battle being waged on the hot Arizona sands. And if we fail—well, then there will be no reason for this writing. There will be none to read it.

The bird is not the greatest of our fears. If when it comes from Venus it finds here a quiet, lifeless, unresponsive shell, it will move outward—we believe and pray—to Mars, then Jupiter, and thence beyond.

That is the end we hope to bring about. Soon, now, our probing needles will penetrate Earth's shell, will dip beneath the crust and into the tegument of that horror which sleeps within us.

But we have another more tormenting fear. It is that before the mother bird approaches us the fledgling may awake and seek to gain its freedom from the shell encasing it. If this should happen, Abramson has warned, our work must then proceed at lightning speed. For let that fledgling once begin to knock, then it must die—or all mankind is doomed.

That is the other reason why I write. To keep from thinking thoughts I dare not think. Because:

Because early this morning, Earth began to knock. . . .

# The Smile of the Sphinx

## by William F. Temple

### The Sphinx

*I gaze across the Nile; flamelike and red*
*The sun goes down, and all the western sky*
*Is drowned in sombre crimson; wearily*
*A great bird flaps along with wings of lead,*
*The sky is hard green bronze, beneath me lie*
*The sleeping ships; there is no sound, or sigh*
*Of the wind's breath,—a stillness of the dead.*

*Over a palm tree's top I see the peaks*
*Of the tall pyramids; and though my eyes*
*Are barred from it, I know that on the sand*
*Crouches a thing of stone that in some wise*
*Broods on my heart; and from the darkening land*
*Creeps Fear and to my soul in whispers speaks.*

—Alfred Lord Douglas

## I

It was past midnight when I went tearing along the Dover Road in my two-seater, at fifty miles an hour, to meet the strangest adventure of my life on the summit of Shooter's Hill. But that lay twenty minutes ahead in the future, and I was as unsuspecting of it as a traveler in the Dover Coach, a century and a half ago, was unaware of the highwayman lying in ambush somewhere on this same road.

Personally, I had no business to be on that road that night, for it is hardly the direct route to Salisbury. I was returning from an East Coast holiday, and had gone a good deal out of my way to cover Shooter's Hill. But I had been reading *A Tale of Two Cities* on my vacation, and the opening scene was so vivid in my memory that my confounded romanticism—I write historical novels for a living—had to be satisfied.

The road, no longer mire, but hard and darkly shining under the eerie blue mercury-vapor lamps (I wondered; what would Dickens have thought of those lamps?), led me up past the massive water-tower that looks like a tall Norman castle, up to the very summit of the hill. I braked then, and pulled the car into the curb a few yards down.

An hour's driving had brought on stiffness, and here was the time and place to stretch my legs. There was not a soul in sight, and the road ran emptily away into a string of blue lights, towards the horizon and London. I extricated myself, and lit a cigarette, meditatively eyeing the dark woods that fringed this side of the road.

Although the moon was high in a cloudless sky, the woods looked too thick and gloomy for a pleasant stroll. So I sauntered across the road, and came to the head of a narrow lane that sloped down towards Woolwich. Constitution Hill, it was called.

There was an old mansion on the right; the windows behind its portico were shuttered. Farther down was a railed-in, grassy space, containing a few trees. It had once been part of the mansion's grounds, and was now the only part not built upon. The rest of the grounds was covered with a vast housing estate that stretched all down the hill. I stood on a corner and surveyed the view.

Two miles away, and below, an arm of the Thames lay across the middle distance like a strip of dull metal. Street lamps pricked the darkness in Woolwich, but the familiar neon signs did not—the cinemas and public-houses had long shut their doors for the night. The low buildings of the great Arsenal, which ran for miles along the river bank, were indistinguishable from the rest of the shadowy blur of Woolwich. Across the river, an immense derrick showed its head above the dockyards and the grey vagueness of Essex, and from this distance it looked like a very small toy.

Of all the houses of the estate before me, I could not see one with a lighted window. All the town was asleep and dreaming, and I stood there on the corner like the last living inhabitant of this world. It occurred to me how awful a fate that would be, were it true—the loneliness, the intimidating silence, the absence of any response or hope of it. And then, to spoil the illusion, came a distant shout from somewhere down the hill.

I looked down the steep road, but could see nobody. The faint shout came again. "Woe!" it sounded like. "Woe!"

I looked more narrowly, and then it seemed that the inky shadow of one of the houses down there had detached itself, and was advancing up the moonlit street towards me. Yes, it was moving! A strange black shadow on the ground, steadily approaching. . . .

It gave me something of a qualm. I turned to retreat to my car, then hesitated out of sheer curiosity. On sudden impulse, I clambered up the base of the nearest lamp-standard, and waited, hanging there uneasily. Now I could discern some little human figures far down the hill, behind the long, black shadow. They were shouting and laughing. I felt relieved. It could not be so bad.

The dark mass on the ground approached swiftly and silently, and resolved itself into a herd of little bodies. Green eyes began to glint amongst them. A plague of large rats? I leaned over, peering intently, as the leaders of the herd came into the light cast by the lamp above my head.

They were *cats*! Hundreds of them, of all shapes and sizes. Led by three big, black toms—one had white paws—they swept past me in a slinky, undulating wave, covering every inch of the road and footpath, parting to pass my lamp-standard, and joining again into a compact mass.

Tabbies there were, Siamese and tailless Manx, fat, bushy Persians and hosts of the common breed, some with kittens in their mouths. They ignored me completely, and casting never a glance aside, pressed forward with an apparently common and urgent purpose, up the hill, past the decrepit mansion, towards the Dover Road. Their small, padded feet made no sound on the tarmac, and not a kitten so much as mewed.

" 'S'truth!" I murmured, rather inelegantly for a literary man, while the feline multitude thronged past like a Chinese army. At last the rear came in sight, together with a dozen or so human beings, who had happened upon this strange phenomenon and were following it with eager curiosity.

There were some lively town lads amongst them, who kept trying to grab the tails of the last few cats—there were no actual stragglers—and pull them back. "Whoa!" they shouted boisterously. "Whoa!" But I noticed that the cats always eluded their clutches, and hastened on.

The end of the procession swept rapidly past, and had vanished over the brow of the hill before I had lowered myself from my perch. I almost trod on the toes of an old man in a slouch cap who had dropped out of the chase. He leaned against the standard, panting.

"In a 'ell of a 'urry, ain't they?" he gasped, jerking his thumb up the hill. "Cor'!"

"Yes," I said. "What's it all about?"

"Damdifino. All the ruddy cats in Woolwich seem to 'ave taken it into their 'eads to leave 'ome. My Lizzie's there—somewhere. Jumped aht the bedroom winder."

"Have you any idea as to where they're going?"

"To the woods, I bet. Yus; to the woods, o' course." He chuckled, and winked at me.

"Beats me," I said, shaking my head and turning away. "I think I'll go and see what's left of my car."

"Hi!"

I turned again. It was not the cockney but a uniformed constable, mounting the hill in lengthy strides. He came up to us. "Seen anything out of the ordinary along here?" he questioned abruptly.

"Not 'arf we ain't," chuckled the cockney. " 'Bout fifty fousand cats gorn up there, mate."

The constable looked sharply at me. I nodded. "He's right, strange as it sounds. They're probably all over in the woods by now."

"I was told something like that by a man down the road," said the policeman. "Well, I suppose I'll have to go and dig out whatever's at the bottom of it all." He walked quickly on.

"Promises to be interesting," I remarked. "I think—"

I stopped, as a tremendous flash of white light leapt into the sky over Woolwich. For a split second, the landscape for miles around stood out clearly, weirdly lit by a pale, quivering glare. And then the night plunged down again, darker than before.

For a moment, my confused mind struggled with this new phenomenon. Then a fierce, orange plume of flame suddenly spurted up from somewhere in the same direction, cleaving the night sky in twain. Silently it jumped and flickered over the Arsenal buildings, while thick, black smoke boiled up from its base, and a reflection of it danced redly in the waters of the Thames. It seemed tall from this distance: down there in Woolwich it must have looked a fearful height.

"Gor' blimey, the Arsenal's on fire!" croaked the cockney excitedly. And at that moment the noise of the first explosion reached us; a battering crash of sound that smashed half the windows in the estate, shook the ground so that I bit my tongue with the concussion, and knocked me deaf, sick, and dizzy.

I remember that I reeled about for a space, with my

hands over my ears, in a state of blind confusion, and recovered to see that the flame over the Arsenal now had eight companions, twisted towers of fire spanning its entire length. Some high cloud-mist in the heavens glared in sympathy with the flames, and reflected them, so that the whole northern hemisphere was an awesome sight, like a tremendous bowl-fire glowing down on earth. And reaching vertically up into the heart of it was a mighty column of dense black smoke, a pillar of hell.

The heavy rumble of explosions was continuous, and periodic, sharper detonations almost split our eardrums. They had been heaping up the shells down there, and now the fireworks had started in earnest. Electric-blue flashes played like lightning around the bases of the great flames, and the debris which they threw up rose in showers of black dots against the throbbing furnace light.

Some of these flying fragments began to hum about us, and slush their way through the leafy branches of the few trees. I became aware that the constable had returned, and was standing beside the cockney; and both their faces were florid with the glare. Suddenly there was an almighty crash up the road: a hurtling mass of machinery had caught the water-tower squarely and piled it into rubble across the ancient highway.

The constable shouted something that I could not catch above the din. He pointed down the hill, and I saw a wall of smoke billowing up towards us. It came swiftly, and there was no escape. In a second it was over us, and we were in a dense, sulphurous fog that made us cough and choke and run at the eyes.

Our surroundings were now veiled in a murky obscurity, and even the eruption in Woolwich was but a diffused glow in the mist ahead. I think I would have made my way back to my car then, had it not been for the action of the constable. He obviously entertained no thought of retiring, but clasped his handkerchief over his mouth and nose, and set off through the smoke-wreaths down Constitution Hill. His duty lay in Woolwich, and he would get there somehow.

The cockney, stifling a paroxysm of coughing, jerked his thumb after the policeman and looked at me inquiringly. Feeling suddenly ashamed of my lack of spirit, I nodded vigorously, and caught his arm.

We started off through the whirling smoke-screen after the dim figure ahead, and came up with him in a clear patch of air. If it hadn't been for those occasional rifts in the smoke, we should have suffocated. The three of us gulped fresh air for a few moments, then plunged on again, until at last we descended into the stricken town.

## II

The next act of this strange and swift drama came on the following evening. From where I reclined in a deck-chair beside my lonely cottage—it was three miles to the nearest dwelling—the tremendous expanse of Salisbury Plain rolled out to meet a red-gold sunset. The sky was a darkening blue above, and smeared in the east with salmon-pink cloud-wisps.

I lay and stared at the slowly changing shapes and colors of the clouds tumbled around the departing sun, and gently stroked the grey, furry body of my cat, Peter, who was curled up and dozing on my lap. He had spent the last fortnight in a home in Salisbury, and hadn't left my side since I picked him up on the way back from Woolwich.

I looked down at him, and noticed my hands again. Scratched and bruised they were, with skinned knuckles and torn fingernails, and now and then they trembled uncontrollably.

Visions of last night kept floating between me and the sunset, and I could not put them out of my mind. Things had happened so much in a rush that I'd had little time to ponder on them; but now, spoiling my attempt to rest, it was all coming back.

The streets of houses shattered and burning, looking far worse than many bombing raids I had seen, and the moans of the poor souls imprisoned in and under them. The frantic tearing with bare hands to extricate the tortured victims before the arrival of the eager, untamable flames, and the sickening horror of failure, when one rushed madly away from a scene too appalling to witness. The clanging fire-engines and ambulances, and the tear-stained faces of lost children and bereaved others.

All this in a choking, dust-laden atmosphere, every particle of which jumped and quivered with the detonations of the unceasing barrage in the Arsenal, and seen only in the blood-red light of flames. For the whole town had lain under the shadow of a pall of black smoke, which blotted out the sky like an immense raven's wing, so that none could tell when morning came. Ever and again, shapeless things of steel and concrete dropped like thunderbolts out of the jet heavens, and sometimes molten metal, and sometimes part of once-living creatures. . . .

A faint breeze came rippling over the grass of the plain, and stirred the newspapers at my feet. They were late morning editions, black with headlines describing the scenes in Woolwich. There was a brief interview in one of them with myself—a few sentences I had jerked out to a reporter while bandaging the broken shoulder of a little boy:

"Mr. Eric Williams, the well-known novelist, who saw the whole thing from Shooter's Hill and immediately rushed down to help in the rescue work, mentions a queer sight which he witnessed just before the first explosion in the Arsenal. A procession of hundreds of cats . . ."

In the stop press columns were hints of perhaps even stranger news. Munition factories had been, and still were, blowing up all over the world. Springfield, Illinois, was a smoldering wreck. Ammunition dumps left over from the war were going off like jumping crackers all over Europe. There were rumors of such things happening in Russia—the Soviet government would release no definite information, but it seemed that there was consternation beyond the Urals.

The most significant item was one smudged sentence, stamped in crookedly and hastily at the foot of the column: "The U.S. atomic research center at Oak Ridge, Tennessee, has been almost totally destroyed by fire."

Sabotage, I reflected. But sabotage on such a large and indiscriminate scale that it must be the work of a tremendously powerful and marvelously organized international secret society of militant pacifists, seeking to save man from himself.

Deep in speculation, I raised my eyes from the paper and gazed again at the glorious painting of the sunset. And there, black against it, far out on the plain, was the little figure of someone cycling steadily in my direction. The person was approaching along a hardly discernible track over the grass, and presently I saw that it was a middle-aged man in a sports jacket.

He dismounted at the rough palings of my fence, regarded me for a moment, then called: "Excuse me, but does your name happen to be Williams—Mr. Eric Williams?" I nodded, and he said he wished to speak to me for a few minutes.

"Certainly, but it's no use trying to sell me anything," I replied, eyeing with suspicion a brown attaché case strapped to the carrier of his cycle.

"Oh, I'm not a salesman," he said, propping his cycle against the gatepost and advancing up the short path. "I would just—" He broke off as he noticed Peter on my lap. He had brown, very tired-looking eyes, and there was an odd, irresolute expression in them at the moment. "I would just like some information," he went on, recovering, and seating himself rather gingerly on the lawn beside me.

"Go ahead," I said, curiously.

He removed his old hat, revealing a large, bald head, fringed with greying hair. He jerked a couple of newspapers from his pocket, and indicating one, said:

"This interview with you. About what you saw on Shooter's Hill . . ." He breathed deeply and paused.

"Yes?" I asked.

He rounded on me suddenly. His brown eyes were agonized. "For God's sake!" he blurted. "Please take that cat away! I—I can't bear them near me. I know it's silly; but, really, the sight of them upsets my nerves."

I arose quietly and carried Peter to the front door of the

cottage, dropped him inside and shut the door. The stranger apologized incoherently as I sat down again.

"It's quite all right," I said. "I know several people who share your phobia. Why, the old Duke of Wellington, although he conquered Napoleon, was scared stiff of cats—wouldn't go into a room where there was one."

"Yes, subconsciously, he was aware of the incredible truth," muttered the stranger. "How fortunate for him he didn't realize it more fully."

I didn't get the drift of this, and he saw that I didn't, and went on in a more matter-of-fact tone, gaining confidence now that Peter had gone.

"I should introduce myself. My name is Clarke, and I live in Salisbury. I'm a retired schoolmaster. Lately, I have evolved an unusual theory, and those cats you saw leaving Woolwich last night form a real, corroborative link in my chain of evidence. So I should be glad if you would be good enough to describe the scene in a little more detail than this newspaper paragraph gives."

I obliged, to the best of my ability, describing the silent and purposeful way in which the cats had passed, and mentioning the leaders.

He pondered over this, and remarked: "Doesn't it seem odd to you that they should all leave the town just before the calamity struck it? And that they put the protecting bulwark of a high hill between Woolwich and themselves?"

"You mean that they somehow sensed what was going to happen?" I asked. "I admit that cats, like dogs, are sometimes credited with a sixth sense, but I can't imagine how they could possibly foresee something so—well, so unprecedented as that."

"I am going to say something rather startling, so please don't think I'm out of my wits," he said, slowly. "I say those animals knew the catastrophe in the Arsenal was coming, *because they planned it!*"

I gaped. Then, perceiving that I had a psychological case to deal with after all, passed it off with a mild remark: "Really, do you think so?"

He grasped my reaction immediately, and flushed.

"I see you *do* think I'm a crank. Perhaps you imagine my dislike of cats is some sort of warped hatred, finding expression in blaming every conceivable mishap onto them. Believe me, it is not so. I was very fond of cats—once."

With an unsteady hand, he picked up his other newspaper.

"Have you seen this evening edition? No? Listen to this bit about the Springfield disaster: 'Inhabitants of neighboring towns report that large numbers of cats have taken up residence there. They apparently fled from Springfield last night. The police stations are crowded with the mewing fugitives.' "

I took the paper from him, and read the item through carefully.

"It certainly is odd," I agreed. "Well, what is your theory?"

"This: that all cats are not so innocent as they appear. That they are an ancient and alien race, with intellects far greater than ours. That they are parasites of the human race, and move amongst us as unsuspected spies, hearing, seeing everything we do, yet never betraying themselves in any way. Believe me, they're the world's best actors! They know their role by heart—they've practiced it for thousands of years, and never yet made a slip."

"What could possibly be their motive?" I inquired.

"I do not think there is any evil intent: they are above evil. It just suits their convenience that we should make pets of them and keep their physical bodies alive for them, for their bodies really are only husks— they live their true lives in their minds. But these husks are necessary, for mind must have a living body to keep it supplied with energy.

"The idea of reincarnation actually works for them, too. When a cat's body dies, the mind that inhabited it transfers itself to some newly-born kitten."

"Whoever originated the saying about cats having nine lives must have felt the truth unconsciously," I murmured sarcastically.

"Yes," agreed Clarke. "This process has been going on for many ages. In fact, the race of minds existing in the bod-

ies of cats today is almost identically the same that landed
upon this planet thousands of years ago."

"Landed upon this planet?" I repeated weakly.

Clarke mopped his shining head again.

"Let me give you a brief history of these creatures," he
said. "I don't expect you to believe it, but it's true. Firstly
the moon was inhabited much more recently than some
think. It was shared by two races, the feline and the canine
They were incompatible from the start, and finally a terrific
war broke out between them.

"Now, the feline mind could detach itself at will from
any body—though it could not remain apart from that body
long without its store of energy becoming exhausted—and
these minds were practically indestructible, even if they
happened to be inhabiting a body at the time it was de
stroyed. But there was an Achilles' heel, and the canine race
knew of it. One thing alone could harm a feline mind, and
that was a violent explosion adjacent to it. By 'adjacent' I
mean within a foot, or two at most, for the feline mind is a
tenacious and almost unshakable structure. But a really concentrated effect of disruption slap up against it will somehow upset the balance of forces which holds that incorpore-
al mind together. It disintegrates, and to all intents and
purposes it is finished as an entity forever.

"So the canine race made their first attacks with immense bombs, shells, and land-mines in an effort to blast the
cat intelligences out of existence. It was a hit-and-miss business, and it didn't fare very well. Only near-enough direct
hits affected the cats, and even with the size of the explosives used these were few and practically negligible in number.

"And then the canines discovered the secret of the
atomic bomb. This was a different proposition altogether.
You didn't need direct hits with these. I believe the nature
of the bomb, as distinct from the mere blast of the cruder explosives, had an added effect, too. Anyway, this meant death
from a distance for the cats, and they were nearly wiped
out. You can see yourself how thoroughly the canines

pounded them—those great craters which pit and scar the face of the moon give some idea of the number and size of the bombs used.

"But the ruling mind of the cats, which was the most powerful intellect in this universe, produced a triumph, just in time. It was a long-distance ray which, when turned on the canine creatures, caused a corruption in their thyroid glands, so that they rapidly degenerated into a race of dullards.

"Thus the cat race triumphed, and ruled the moon. But the war had made such havoc of that world—almost all vegetation was destroyed by radioactivity—that food of any sort was scarce. They had to give more and more time to searching for nourishment as the moon grew more barren. This was not to their liking, for, as I've said, they live a life of the mind, and they resented having to waste time and energy in mere food-hunting.

"At last the resourceful ruling mind invented a form of spaceship, and in large numbers of these vessels the entire race migrated to Earth. Here they still are—and we are their unconscious servants . . ."

I have always believed that anything is possible, no matter how improbable, and so I did not immediately scoff at this seemingly wild theory. In fact, I was curious to hear more.

"What became of the mentally weakened canine race?" I asked.

"The larger part of it was left on the moon to perish of starvation. But the cat-people brought some specimens with them, and these flourished and multiplied enormously on this planet, and they still do."

"Do you mean—*dogs* are the descendants of that defeated race?" I asked incredulously.

"Yes. But they have never recovered their original mind-power; beside the cold and vast intellects of the cats, they are just amicable dolts. A remnant of their sixth sense—telepathy—remains, but it is not developed to anything like the intense degree that it has in cats today."

"Perhaps the other old habits also linger in the muddled canine minds," I suggested, suddenly carried away on the wings of this fantasy. "For instance, the hitherto inexplicable enmity between dogs and cats. Dogs chase cats because they have a dim memory that they are old enemies. And I suppose cats allow themselves to be chased to keep up the appearance of innocence?"

"Yes; they're devilish subtle actors. Another old problem is explainable, too. Why do dogs bay at the moon? Simply because the sight of it arouses a vague memory of their old home—they howl with homesickness, though they may not realize it." There followed a short silence, in which I weighed up possibilities.

"About the cats blowing up all these munition works," I ventured. "You think—?"

"I know why. It is obvious. As I have said, atomic bombs spell death to the feline minds. Now, very little of the explosives tossed about in the mud of France in the First World War came anywhere near cats, and they ignored that war. But towards the end of the Second World War they were preparing to intervene.

"Too many of their number were being killed in the heavy air raids. I mean, their *minds* were being killed—not their bodies, because they don't care a damn about that: there are always plenty of fresh ones to move into. But once a mind is disintegrated by explosive, it is finished and not replaceable. Also, food supplies were being totally disorganized, and men—their servants—were everywhere leaving them to fend for themselves: a great distraction from the work they were giving their minds to. But, like the canines, man stumbled upon the atomic bomb, and that finished the war, which satisfied the cats in one way but disturbed them in another.

"Suppose these stupid servants of theirs started another war, but this time rocketing atomic bombs about? Then that would mean destruction for everyone, feline minds included.

"They bided their time to see whether man would have

the plain common sense to see that war was a practice that had become mass lunacy, and that the only way to end war between nations was to end nations by uniting under one world government. Well, we don't, to our eternal shame, as you know.

"So they are effectively nipping the Third World War in the bud, by destroying the tools necessary for it. Men look upon themselves as minds above animals. I'm afraid the truth is that the cats are the minds, and men are just animals."

"H'm." It was certainly an explanation of the strange thing I had seen on Shooter's Hill. But—

"Look here, this theory is taking a hell of a lot of things for granted," I objected. "It cannot be anything but supposition. You have no proof?"

He bit his lip, and began nervously to pluck blades of grass from the lawn.

"No," he admitted. "Nothing tangible, beyond the strange behavior of the cats which you yourself saw. But I tell you I know all I've said is true. I have an odd feeling of certainty now, about my story."

He shivered slightly again, and so did I, for a chill breeze swept in from the plain, and I looked up to find with a mild shock that it was nearly dark. The sun had long since gone, and bright Venus was glittering about the somber night rack.

Clarke scrambled to his feet, and apologized for keeping me so long. I said it had been intensely interesting, and would he drop in again sometime to resume our discussion? He promised he would.

I watched him cycling off into the western dusk, and folding my chair, I turned to take it indoors. And immediately I saw Peter, a shadowy outline against the darkening sky, squatting on the roof of the cottage. He gave me quite a qualm, with such weird thoughts still roaming my mind.

It was obvious how he had escaped. I had converted the one upstairs room of my cottage into an amateur observatory, enlarging the skylight all round to give the four-inch telescope latitude. When I shut Peter in, he had simply gor upstairs and out through this wide window onto the tile He had done that trick before.

I called to him, and he glanced idly down at me. H eyes were shining greenly in the dark.

"Jump, Peter-boy," I called, extending my arms. I ha to repeat it several times before he arose, yawned hugel and stretched lazily, then condescendingly jumped from th gutter into my arms. He commenced to purr softly as I ca ried him indoors.

All the time I was preparing my supper, I kept shootin surreptitious glances at him as he crouched, half asleep, i the big armchair. What Clarke had said about subtle actin recurred to me. Was Peter really watching me? Peter, whor I had reared from a kitten, and who I flattered myself ha some affection for me? Had he come out on that roof behin and above us to eavesdrop—literally?

I rolled him over on his back, and he stretched laz paws up at me. "Brr-ow," he said.

"It's no use, Peter, old man," I said deliberately, pokin his tummy. "You needn't keep on acting. I can see throug you all the time. You're a spy—that's what you are!"

He took not the slightest notice, but lay dreamily ac cepting my caresses. I gave it up, switched on my battery ra dio, and sat down to supper. With a mouth full of bread anc cheese, I heard the late news coming through as the tube warmed up.

". . . great damage, and martial law has been declared ir the city. The president has issued an appeal to the nation tc remain calm. The Federal authorities have the matter wel in hand, he said, and precautions now taken make it impos sible for any further such outrages to occur. From Sweden Denmark, and Northern Italy come reports of widespreac fires in government-controlled laboratories of physical re search. Nearer home, three ammunition dumps in the Welsh hills blew up simultaneously this morning . . ."

There was a good deal more of it, and a late flash that

the rocket testing buildings at Peenemunde had been wiped out in a series of explosions apparently begun by a mishap in an experimental petrol and oxygen mixing chamber.

Although sabotage was suspected in many cases, so far no arrests had been made, because in each instance the eruptions had been so sudden and violent that no human beings in the vicinity had survived to be suspected. It was assumed that either the saboteurs were using time bombs or else they were suicidal fanatics.

For my own part, the fact that no evidence of human activity had been found in any one of all those catastrophes was itself evidence that no human agency was at work here. But whether it was cats or . . . Oh, it was all too fantastic!

I switched the radio off, and decided I would refuse to think any more about the whole business this day.

I sought refuge in a book of short stories from my shelves. It was an admirably written collection by C. E. Montague, called *Action*. In its vivid pages I lost myself until, in a story "Wodjabet," I happened upon a character who "only blinked the way a cat does, letting on that it's sleepy when really its eyes are aglow with some grand private excitement or other . . ."

Which caused me to peep from under my brows across at Peter again.

He was curled up, really asleep. Or was he? . . .

### III

The next morning was bright and fresh, and as I pushed the lawnmower up and down in the sunshine I wondered how I could have been so foolish, on the previous evening, as to consider seriously, even for a moment, the quaint Mr. Clarke's cock-and-bull story. Thus does the normal round reassure us, and melt away the dark underside of our imagination.

Peter was dashing about the lawn like a mad kitten, chasing errant leaves and several times coming near to being churned up by my mower. I paused to watch him, just as a butterfly made its erratic flight into the garden and settled. Peter eyed it eagerly, and approached with stealth. A couple of yards away he stopped, nose down and rear up, quivering all over with the intensity of his purpose.

Suddenly he leapt, and missed the butterfly by an inch. It fluttered drunkenly away, and Peter bounded after it, clawing the air wildly and ineffectively. He wasn't looking where he was going, and smack he went against a water-butt.

I had to laugh. How absurd it was to suspect Peter! Peter, the good-natured—I'm sure that cat had a sense of humor—but Peter, the stupid, who could never learn the simplest of tricks. An amoeba would have beaten him in an intelligence test. All he had ever done was eat, sleep, and play.

I leaned on my mower and ruminated on Peter, who had settled down on a heap of cut grass. Why were cats ever born? What useless lives they led! How the devil did they pass the time, when they could do nothing constructive, physically or mentally? They never even had to hunt for their food, which is the chief occupation and reason for existence of the wild animals. Mostly they just sat about—brooding.

Were they really thinking in those long spells of passivity, or were they just bored stiff? I found myself considering, after all, the arguments that Clarke had raised ...

And suddenly the man's voice broke into my thoughts: "Er—good morning, Mr. Williams."

I turned, and beheld him standing rather awkwardly outside the gate, holding his bicycle.

"Ah, good morning," I said, with a heartiness that was not wholly genuine. "I was just thinking about you."

"Er—I was wondering," he began again, with a nervous eye on Peter, "wondering whether you would care to accompany me on a cycle ride this morning, over the plain? There are some new points I'd like to discuss with you. I noticed you had a cycle, and thought perhaps—"

"Yes, by all means," I said. "It's a lovely morning for it.

Just come inside for a moment, will you, and have a drink while I clean up?"

He came hesitantly into the cottage parlor, making an arc to avoid Peter. It occurred to me that I never saw a man who looked less in need of a cycle ride and more in need of a drink. He looked haggard and careworn, and his eyes were more tired than ever. I poured him a whisky and soda, and left him to it while I had a wash and brush up.

When I returned from the kitchen, there he was slumped in a chair, staring white-faced at the opposite wall. There were wet spots on his coat where he had spilled some of his drink. I followed his gaze, and saw that the center of his interest was a framed photograph of the Sphinx of Gizeh. It was a souvenir brought back from Cairo, through which city I'd passed on my way to join the war in the desert—only then the Sphinx had had its chin propped up with sandbags, and didn't look nearly so romantic as it did in the commercial photograph.

"Hello—whatever's the matter?" I asked.

"N-nothing," he answered, dropping his gaze. "Coincidences can be unsettling sometimes, that's all."

He gulped the rest of his drink, and got up. But he vouch-safed nothing further until we were miles out on the plain, riding slowly side by side towards the monoliths of Stonehenge on the skyline. Then, suddenly, he said: "Do you know why that picture affected me like that?"

I shook my head.

"Because the Sphinx is an image of the Ruling Mind of the feline race. The body is not that of a lion, *but of a great cat!*"

He lapsed into reverie again.

Stonehenge was deserted. The modern road ran over the plain to a bare horizon, and the remains of far more ancient roads and the faint tracks made by the Bronze Age peoples might never have been trodden since the days of those long-departed civilizations. It was not the tourist season, and if there had been any watchers for the dawn, they had gone.

We wheeled our cycles between the massive obelisks

and laid them beside the Altar Stone. I noticed that Clarke's brown bag was still strapped to his carrier. Clarke sat himself on the flat slab, and brooded there like "*The Thinker*," as silent as the stones around us.

I decided not to press for information, but to let it come in its own way. So, irreverently, I struck a match on the Altar Stone, the death-bed (so the stories go) of countless souls who had been sacrificed by the Druids, and squatted down beside him, striving patiently to get my pipe going.

The tobacco caught just as Clarke broke his silence. "I brought you out here so that we could not possibly be overheard," he said. "That cat of yours—I don't trust it."

He paused again in that irritating way of his, then went on: "You remember what I told you about the Ruling Mind of the feline race? Well, it is still alive, still directing their activities, and it is the power behind all these recent happenings. More than that, *it is somewhere very close to me!* "

His voice shook a little. He took out his handkerchief and mopped his almost hairless head.

"I *know* it is very close to me, as surely as I know those other things I told you. And as certainly as I know other things which have become plain to me since. All the time, I am aware of it watching me. In my rooms, in the crowded street, in empty lanes and fields, in the cinema—everywhere I go, I can feel that the Mind is somewhere very near. Even now—"

He looked almost apprehensively around at the order and disorder of the big stones, and the sweep of the plain. But apart from some bird in flight away to the east, there was no indication of any living thing.

"I cannot understand," he said, huskily. "It must be occupying a body of some sort. Even that Mind can't exist for long without physical nourishment. But what—or who? I regard every animal I see with suspicious fear. Sometimes I even think it may have taken command of some *human* body. That milkman who spoke to me this morning may have been only a masquerader, and behind his smile—"

"You shouldn't pay any attention to thoughts of that

kind," I said. "It will develop into a phobia; you will be afraid of everybody. And this infallible knowledge of yours— What are the other things you mentioned had since been revealed to you?"

"I know some more of the history of the feline race. It is pictured as clearly in my mind as if I had witnessed it all. If you look at the *Encyclopedia Britannica*—and, in fact, if you study all that is known of the origin of the cats—you will find that they suddenly appear in one country, and one alone—Egypt. That is where *felis domestica* first enters into our knowledge. Why? Because that is where the feline spaceships from the moon landed thousands of years ago."

"I know the ancient Egyptians regarded cats as supernatural beings," I mused. "They worshiped them, made statues of them. It was a crime to kill a cat, wasn't it?"

"Yes," said Clarke, absently. "The penalty was very severe. In fact, when the King of Persia invaded Egypt, the spearhead of his army was a group of soldiers carrying cats in their arms. The Egyptians were so terrified of harming the animals that they submitted tamely to defeat."

"Usen't they to embalm the bodies of cats and bury them in the holy city of Bubastes?" I asked. "They're still finding them, hundreds of their mummified bodies. Why, only the other day—"

But Clarke was not listening. "The remains of those spaceships are still there in Egypt, covered by the sands of the desert," he muttered. "I could lead you to them."

"That would be tangible proof at last," I said.

"The feline and Egyptian races more or less adopted each other," went on Clarke. "The Egyptians worshiped the strange invaders as near-gods, and appreciated their high intelligence, even though they understood little of it. They offered up food to the cats, and kept them in their houses and temples. Naturally, after the hardships of the moon, the cats took kindly to this life. At last they could relax from the pressing preoccupation of searching for food, and devote their time to thought."

"Regarding this life of thought—" I began; but Clarke

had got under way now, and he went ahead like a gramo-
phone, perhaps fearful that if he stopped he might not be
able to start again.

"One reason immensely increased the reverence of the
Egyptians for the cats: the discovery that they were, in reality, deathless spirit-minds inhabiting transient bodies. The
Egyptians soon based their whole religion on this—that's
where they got their famous belief in the immortality of the
spirit, its life after death, and possible reincarnation.

"The rite of mummifying the worn-out husks of the
cats symbolized the eternal life of the feline minds, and the
Egyptians extended this to embalming their own dead—and
hoping. They took the emblem of the feline race, the *crux
ansata*, and regarded it as the symbol of life.

"For a long time the two races lived in this fashion of
mutual convenience. The Egyptians knew there was a Ruling Mind of the cats, though its location and appearance was
a mystery to them. But they built the Sphinx in its honor,
and to represent the harmony of the two races, gave its cat's
body the head of their reigning Pharaoh.

"The Egyptians derived a few ideas from the cats and
their old lunar civilization, particularly methods of building, metalwork, and decoration, some of which even our
modern scientists have failed to rediscover. Malleable glass,
imperishable enamels, the ever-burning lamps so often mentioned in the literary fragments of the time, and some
miraculous way of reducing precious stones to fluid state
and remolding them.

"But actually there was little intellectual intercourse.
The Egyptians were not equal to grasping even the simplest
conceptions of the feline mind, and the cats had no intention of trying to educate a race which they regarded as being
hardly above the lower animals.

"The cats, you must remember, have none of the
warmth and generosity of humanity: they are, and always
have been, coldly logical, and their main interest is self-pres-
ervation, whatever guise or ruse they adopt to that end.

"For instance, when Egypt became entangled in wars, a

great proportion of the cats migrated to other countries, and left the Egyptian civilization to decay. They thought it wise, too, to let the knowledge of their existence fade from the mind of man with the decline of the Egyptians. For they foresaw that man's intelligence would grow again, and become a keen, questioning probe and a constant interruption in their work. Only in his ignorance would they have peace.

"At first, they suppressed all reference to themselves. The cat is not mentioned once in the Bible, though the dog is many times, and this might be considered strange, for Egypt was next door to the Holy Land. But that is the reason.

"However, they got the idea later that it was better to suppress only the knowledge of their being super-minds, and then they could mix with mankind again and be looked after without being bothered by investigations into their work.

"Britain was one country they came to where their real identity was unknown, but even so they managed to influence men and women to protect them. In A.D. 900—you may look it up—there was a law passed forbidding the wilful murder of any cat. And in the *Ancren Riwle*, the book of rules for nuns written in the 13th century, was the injunction: 'Ye shall not possess any beast, my dear sisters, *except only a cat.*' "

He fell silent again.

"You mention their work," I ventured. "Can you describe this mysterious 'life of the mind'?"

"Well," he answered, "the cats' minds are like a multitude of cells—"

His face, all of a sudden, went ghastly pale. His brown eyes were horror-struck; his mouth opened and shut in silent gasps.

"What's up?" I cried.

"I—I—If I thought—" he gulped, then whispered tremulously: "No, I must not believe that!"

I regarded this enigma of a man with detached curiosity for a moment. I had never come across such a bundle of nerves. It occurred to me that if I had to put up with this proneness to sudden nervous attacks much longer I should become jumpy myself.

He produced a hip-flask, and promptly choked over a mouthful of undiluted spirit. But it took effect, and presently he mopped his head again and resumed, in a slightly thicker voice:

"A multitude of cells are working independently, but in telepathic communication with each other. The Ruling Mind, though, is in constant contact with all of them at once, and sorts and correlates their thoughts and reasonings, fitting them together to get the whole aspect. They have no need of books or pens: their infallible memories are their only records. No need to travel: they can cast their minds over great distances. No need of materials: they balance and control the forces of nature with the unsupported force of their own minds.

"But one force has so far beaten them—they cannot master the activity behind the chemical change of metabolism. It is the major problem they have in hand. You see, they don't like being dependent on energy from food to sustain their bodies, which in turn sustain the brain cells they must use to keep up their life of thought. So they are seeking other ways of getting that energy—so far, without success.

"You know," he went on, "there is much to envy in their mode of living. Many of our own philosophers have come to the conclusion that research workers, engrossed in their work, probably live the happiest and most satisfying life of all. The cats believe that, too. Their life is an infinite adventure into the unknown, solving intriguing problems and puzzles, their interest sustained by the promise of unbounded novelties to come.

"It is a pleasurable and absorbing hunt for fundamental truth. What are our vanities and posings, our squabbles and out-smarting, beside that great search? We are as worthless as a cloud of gnats."

"Do you know any of the other problems receiving their attention?"

"Mostly they are beyond my comprehension," he said. "Especially their stupendously advanced mathematics. But I could mention investigations into the strange fibre life on the second planet of the companion of Sirius, into the minute organisms which infest and corrupt typhoid bacteria, into the structure of individual suns in island universes thousands of light-years beyond the reach of our most powerful telescope, into the newly-discovered Law of the Three Probabilities of the Future, and into the cause—"

BOOM! BOOM! BOOM!

We jerked our heads round, to see three mushrooms of white smoke standing on a low hill across the plain. Slowly their heads uncoiled and expanded, and they merged into one shapeless cloud.

Then again: BOOM! A whole row of fresh mushrooms sprang out of the earth almost simultaneously, running in a line towards us.

We jumped up in alarm, and as if our action had caused it, another row of explosions. went streaking across the plain, and this time we glimpsed the red flashes in the heart of them.

"The cats again!" I yelled to Clarke above the uproar. He nodded dazedly, staring at the jumping clouds of smoke and dust. He made an answer which I could not catch.

The thunderous noise grew worse; it was like an intense shell barrage. Were they shells, coming from some unseen guns on the artillery ranges beyond Larkhill? I caught Clarke's eye again.

"Where the hell are they coming from?" I shrieked. He pointed down at the trembling ground, and mouthed: "Below!"

A series of thuds like hammer-blows, from somewhere quite near, jarred us almost physically. It was difficult to locate the explosions that had caused them, for the pallid, whirling wall of a smoke-screen lay across that way, and the thick pillars of the ancient temple stood between it and us like a stockade. I pointed at the open, untouched expanse behind us, and indicated that we must retreat across it.

"We'll have—" I began, and instantaneously a whole acre of the stretch at which my finger pointed squirted itself up like a huge, white oil-gusher—it was almost pure chalk— which balanced there for a split second, then exploded in midair. It was as if someone had burst a great bag of flour. The air was full of white particles flying before the sound-waves of a concussion which equaled that first mighty explosion in Woolwich Arsenal.

The ground seemed to rise in a wave beneath our feet, and I remember that as I went sprawling backwards I caught a glimpse of one of the pillars of Stonehenge lurching out of the vertical, and the slab that had rested upon it falling corner-wise to the earth. The thump of that block landing was the last shock of the mad tattoo.

Silence descended abruptly, and I became conscious that my ears were tingling almost unbearably. I picked myself up shakily. Clarke was in the act of doing likewise.

"Gosh, look at that!" I said, and my voice sounded faint and far away because of my deafness.

"That" was the immense dust-cloud which hung over and veiled half the plain, drifting and changing and mounting tenuously towards the zenith.

"I'll never be able to get through that," I said. "I think I'd better come back with you to Salisbury and wait until it's settled a bit."

Clarke nodded. He had fallen into one of his periods of taciturnity again, and remained so throughout the ride back. But I managed to get one piece of information from him.

"What did you mean by saying those explosions came from below?" I asked.

"There are subterranean caves running for miles underneath the plain," he said shortly. "Few people know of them. The government does. They used them during the war for storing explosives, for safety in air raids."

"And, of course, the Ruling Mind touched them off?"

He nodded sharply again, and shut up like a clam. By his furrowed brow I could see that he was cogitating deeply, and from his expression I saw that the thoughts were not pleasant.

We had a solemn tea in Salisbury, while the street outside was alive with yelling newsboys and excited, arguing people. "Long range rockets, that's what they were..." I caught, and "...knocked Stonehenge down like a row of ninepins."

We had a short walk, pushing our cycles and talking, and we parted by the cathedral. That scene remains in my mind in every detail. The spire tapering to a fine point four hundred feet above our heads, and Clarke's last words before I went my way, enunciated almost pedantically:

"As long as the cats keep up their acting with such infallible assurance, there will always remain an element of doubt in even the most credulous human mind. That little crumb of self-distrust is what will save them. And, believe me, the cats know it!"

It was late evening when I reached my cottage by a circuitous route. The craters were pretty numerous around my way, and the settling chalk-dust covered the torn earth like a thin layer of snow.

A scared-looking Peter was waiting for me on the doorstep. He was jumpy and nervous, and it looked as though the upheaval had nearly frightened him out of his wits. I let him in with peculiarly mixed feelings.

## IV

I found it hard to get to sleep that night. A queer unease possessed me. I felt that something strange and terrible was going to happen soon, and I had no idea what the nature of the thing could be. I lay fidgeting and constantly turning, finding neither bodily nor mental peace.

And then there came a wail, like a sick baby's, outside the window. I sat up, startled.

Silence.

Came another wail, sobbing up the scale to an extremely high pitch. It descended rapidly to a throaty growl, and then a familiar "Mee-ow."

It was only Peter. He had wandered out again after supper. I'd never heard him giving tongue in the night before like this, because other cats rarely strayed out this way. But there was another cat there tonight, for presently she answered. She had a remarkable range: thin shrieks, mournful howls, and an individual, staccato series of noises like an outboard motor.

A most painful duet presently began. I lay and listened to it with interest rather than annoyance. How would Clarke have explained it? No doubt he would have said it was a cunning psychological ruse, to impress the notion in the subconscious mind of man that cats were indeed only animals, having the customary sexual and courting instincts.

If that were true, and it was all acting, then it was indeed finesse! I could not imagine the feline race carrying things so far, but perhaps, as Clarke had said, this acting had become an almost unconscious habit with them, requiring no effort.

My mind played with other explanations. Suppose these outbursts were the more artistic souls of the felines giving expression to their love of music! Were those weird sounds, so discordant to our ears, feline songs of great beauty?

Certainly I had heard Chinese songs that sounded somewhat similar. But I could not accept this explanation, for I could not imagine the cat race having any sort of emotions. All art springs from the emotions, and if Clarke's story were true, those intellects were too cold and logical to waste time on music or any other of the art forms.

In the midst of such speculations, I fell into a doze.

The next day was pure idleness. I could not concentrate on anything, though a half-finished story lay in my drawer. I pottered about, reading snatches of books and papers, listening to the radio, and for the most part just reclining in my deck-chair on the lawn, meditating.

Sunset came—an unusually glorious one. The fine dust

thrown up by the explosions of yesterday was still drifting in the upper atmosphere, and producing an effect similar to those after the famous Krakatoa eruption. The western sky abounded in color, in streaks, flames, wedges, and mists. I wished I had a camera that could catch and preserve the beauty of the scene.

I watched it greedily, half-fearful of the dulling that would presently overcome and dissolve it.

And then, just as he had first entered into my life, the tiny black silhouette of Clarke on his cycle appeared out there on the plain. He was winding his way slowly between the dark ovals of the craters which had obliterated parts of the old grass track, and it was some time before he reached my gate.

He dismounted clumsily, and almost fell over. I got up and went to help him, smiling. But I stopped smiling when I saw his face. It was grey, and moist with sweat, and the dark circles under his eyes had grown more pronounced during the night.

I took the bicycle from his trembling hands, and leaned it against the fence. The strap around the brown case on the carrier was loose. I tightened it automatically, and took Clarke's arm. He leaned on me, drawing little shuddering gasps now and then as I helped him along to the house.

"Take it easy," I said.

"My God!" he muttered. "My God!"

He seemed on the verge of hysteria. The fellow was a constant puzzle to me; he seemed to have so many personalities. The nervous inquirer, the almost rudely terse man, the didactic schoolmaster—and now this shaking wreck. I wondered whether he could possibly be a drug addict.

He lowered himself uncertainly into my armchair and rested his head on his hand. I poured a neat whisky, and had to help him get it down his throat. He lay back.

"Be all right—in a minute," he breathed.

Peter was curled up on the hearthrug. For a few moments he had watched the visitor with faint curiosity, but now his interest had waned and his eyes were closed in sleep again. Apparently . . . I grabbed him up in two handfuls, intending to put him outside, but Clarke stopped me with a weak gesture.

"Doesn't matter now," he murmured. "He knows all about it, anyway."

I sank into the opposite chair, and waited. Until, at length, Clarke began his strangest narrative yet, in broken sentences punctuated with sighs and sometimes uncontrolled invocations to the Almighty.

At first, there was a lot of physiological stuff about the structure of brain-cells, which he rushed through too rapidly for me to grasp properly. But I remember he said that the average person uses only a small percentage of his brain-cells in his lifetime, the larger proportion remaining underdeveloped and unused. He made fleeting references to schizophrenia, "split minds," and enlarged upon the question of multiple personalities.

This last was due, he said, to the brain-cells forming in two or three separate groups, instead of the one whole. Thus, one man's brain could contain two or three totally different minds, each with its own independent memories and reactions, yet each drawing its energy from the same bloodstream.

And something of the sort, only far worse, had happened to him. When he had mentioned the word "cells" yesterday, at Stonehenge, some idea of the terrible truth had dawned upon him. Now, after a sleepless night and day, he was sure that he had found the answer.

No wonder he had felt the strange presence of the Ruling mind so constantly. *It was occupying the larger part of his own brain!*

At this amazing assertion, I just sat gaping at him. In looking back at the whole affair, I don't think I had taken Mr. Clarke very seriously up to this point. Admittedly, at times his story had carried me away, but only as one is carried away by a good film. When I had parted from him, the impression had faded each time, as the characters in a film cease to be real after one has emerged from the cinema into the solid life of the street.

As an author myself, whose work it was to spend half my life in a fictitious world, I knew how easy it was sometimes to confuse that world with fact. I'm afraid I must have looked upon Clarke as an expert weaver of fantasies all this time. I had taken him for one of those involved psychological cases, full of repressions, complexes, escapism, and all that jargon. In short, a queer fish who had swum into my life to entertain me for a while, and provide an interesting passage in my autobiography, when that amusing volume came to be written.

But now it came to me with quite a shock of realization that the man sitting huddled in the opposite chair was *not* dramatizing himself, but genuinely believed in the astounding things he had said, and was overcome by the horror of them.

I gazed at the top of his bald and shining head, and tried to imagine a complex and utterly foreign brain working beside his in that cranium. My imagination boggled.

Clarke slowly raised his head again, and looked up at me. His eyes were red and bleared from lack of sleep. He spoke in a strained, but steadier voice.

"Maybe that's how I knew the things I did. There must have been a leakage of knowledge, filtering through from the pirated brain-cells into my own. Perhaps through the bloodstream; perhaps because such a powerful radiating instrument, in proximity to my own, stimulated my telepathic powers, made my mind more receptive. I was sure the information in my mind was correct, though I couldn't understand where it came from."

"Yes—yes," I stammered. "I suppose that's it."

He went on bitterly: "And the reason for my chronic fatigue—this damned parasite is draining my energy. To think that the thing has always been with me! Why, when we went out to Stonehenge to escape it, it was there all the time with us, overhearing everything. Not that I expect it paid us much heed . . . And it was simple for it, with its complete control of electrical forces, to create a spark in just the right place in those caves under the plain. Just as all the other places were blown up or set on fire."

A gust of rage seized him. "If I could get my hands on it! If only I could get my hands on it!"

The spasm passed. "It must be overhearing me now," he said, wearily.

I felt it was up to me to say something.

"Well, there it is," I said hesitantly. "What on earth are we to do about it?"

He jumped up so suddenly that I started. His unstable emotions boiled over in another flood of rage. His face was convulsed.

"I'm going to do something," he gritted. "I won't be used like this. What's my life become? Another week—another day—of this, and I'll be insane!"

He snatched up his dingy hat ferociously, and made for the door. He was not too steady on his feet, but the intensity of his passion upheld him.

"Good-by, Williams," he flung at me. "I can't tell you anything more. I mustn't even think about it." And he was out and down the path before I could comprehend his swift words.

I followed hurriedly. "Wait," I called. "What—?" But he had mounted his cycle and was already riding away, the bag on his carrier at the rear bumping up and down in derisive farewell.

I stopped at the gate, looking after him. He was shouting as he rode, and the words came back more and more faintly as he dwindled into the distance. They were mostly blasphemy. . . .

I hesitated, and cursed my hesitation. But I could never catch him now: I had been cleaning my bike, and it lay in hopeless dismemberment in the tool-shed. The fellow was very ill. He shouldn't be allowed about like that. He should be under observation.

Observation! An idea suddenly occurred to me. I rushed back into the cottage, almost tripping over Peter, who was coming out of the door, and went clattering up the stairs to my cramped observatory. Sliding the skylight window aside, I swung the telescope window down, and directed it out into the dusk after Clarke.

I looked through it. Everything was a blur, and I fiddled impatiently with the focusing screws. The scene would not come clear. Then: "Fool!" I swore at myself, and delved on the floor for the terrestrial eyepiece.

It was under a heap of star maps. I snatched it out, and with hasty fingers screwed it in place of the astronomical lens. I peered through, and the dark little mote out there between the obscure land and the pale green sky fairly leapt at me, and became the figure of Clarke, dismounted now and crouching on the lip of one of the recent craters.

He was unstrapping the brown bag. I could not see his face, for the brim of his hat shadowed it. He produced a bunch of keys, and used one of them to unlock the case.

I watched with interest, waiting to see what was in that mysterious case. Wads of newspapers—evidently packing—came out first, and then Clarke extracted some sticks—yellow sticks, each about ten inches long.

He put them down and stood up. He gazed around at the darkling plain. He seemed to be undergoing some sort of mental struggle. Then, as if in sudden resolution, he bent swiftly, gathered the sticks in his arms and seemed literally to hurl himself over the rim of the crater.

I gasped as he disappeared from view, for those craters were pretty deep—some went right underground. I waited a minute or two hardly daring to breathe, my eye glued to the spot where he had vanished. His bicycle and the abandoned case were still there on the rim.

Then, without warning, a fountain of dirt, smoke, and flame spurted up from the interior of the crater, catching up and tossing the bicycle fifty yards away and spraying out in a tall, grey plume. Quite slowly, the dust and smaller debris rained down from this erection, and seemed to rebound gently as it landed. A lower layer of white smoke appeared, and rolled along the edge of the crater as if it were a steaming cauldron.

I found that I had bitten my lip, and there was the taste of blood on my tongue. . . .

When I reached the scene twenty minutes later, after a breathless run in the gloom, the cloud had settled, and the crater was nearly half-full of loose debris. It was quite obvious that there was nothing I could do.

Those yellow sticks had been dynamite.

That was a fortnight ago. And now here I sit in my parlor, penning this account of the adventure from beginning to end. I suppose it *is* ended.

Yet could an intelligence of the quality of the Ruling Mind of Clarke's story be trapped by such a trick, even though Clarke did his best to conceal his intention to destroy it through its Achilles' heel—an explosive "slap up against it"? I find that hard to accept.

Certainly, there have been no more explosions since, but that is probably because there is nothing left to explode. Funnily enough, poor Clarke's few sticks of dynamite must have been about the last left upon this planet. As a New York paper said the next day: "There just isn't enough gunpowder left in the world to make a two-cent Fourth of July squib."

Nor was a single plant for manufacturing atom bombs anything but completely gutted walls. Nobody could have taught the cats anything about incendiarism.

Throughout this narrative, I have endeavored to confine it to personal experience only, hardly touching upon the broader events of this global annihilation of the stuff of war. For that is history.

We know now the all-round sense of relief that has come to the peoples of the world. The pact that has been signed to keep the world in its weaponless condition, and to outlaw arms races, may well be the foundation stone of that common world government, after all. Perhaps now the vicious circle has been broken for us, we shall maintain the good sense not to get caught in another.

In any case, if Clarke's story was true, an atomic war will never be able to get started. The feline race will see to that. *If* Clarke's story was true . . .

I always come back to that "if." When I try to sum it all up, doubt defeats me. It is so fantastically far-fetched. I cannot make up my mind whether Clarke was a martyr, or an obsessed lunatic who committed suicide in a remarkably complicated way.

And yet, you know, there are Clarke's own words.... *"As long as the cats keep up their acting with such infallible assurance, there will always remain an element of doubt in even the most credulous human mind. That little crumb of self-distrust is what will save them. And, believe me, the cats know it!"*

It is sunset again, that seemingly fateful time of day in this story. The mellowing rays steal in through the diamond panes of the windows, and there is a golden patch of light moving gently on the opposite wall. There are spots of shadow in it, giving it the effect of a mask. It seems to grin. I look across at Peter squatting on the arm of the chair in which Clarke sat on his last visit. He is in a semi-doze; his eyes are almost, but not quite, shut, and he is purring very softly. There is a look of complacent felicity about him. Is that really a smile on his face? I am sure it is—as much as a cat can smile.

He is crouching like a little sphinx, and my gaze lifts to the framed photograph hanging on the wall above him. The Sphinx of Gizeh—maybe a stone image of the Ruling Mind.

The dread thought occurs to me again. If the strange being left Clarke's body in time before he blew himself to smithereens, it must by now be occupying some other body. It could not remain disembodied long. *Where has it gone?*

I look across at a mirror, and study my head uneasily. For the Lord's sake, not that! My gaze returns to the Sphinx. I scrutinize its battered features.

What an enigmatic expression! Is it a smile?

# Dolphin's Way

## by Gordon R. Dickson

Of course, there was no reason why a woman coming to Dolphin's Way—as the late Dr. Edwin Knight had named the island research station—should not be beautiful. But Mal had never expected such a thing to happen.

Castor and Pollux had not come to the station pool this morning. They might have left the station, as other wild dolphins had in the past--and Mal nowadays carried always with him the fear that the Willernie Foundation would seize on some excuse to cut off their funds for further research. Ever since Corwin Brayt had taken over, Mal had known this fear. Though Brayt had said nothing. It was only a feeling Mal got from the presence of the tall, cold man. So it was that Mal was out in front of the station, scanning the ocean, when the water-taxi from the mainland brought the visitor.

She stepped out on the dock, as he stared down at her. She waved as if she knew him, and then climbed the stairs from the dock to the terrace in front of the door to the main building of the station.

"Hello," she said, smiling as she stopped in front of him. "You're Corwin Brayt?"

Mal was suddenly sharply conscious of his own lean and ordinary appearance in contrast to her startling beauty. She was brown-haired and tall for a girl—but these things did not describe her. There was a perfection to her—and her smile stirred him strangely.

"No," he said. "I'm Malcolm Sinclair. Corwin's inside."

"I'm Jane Wilson," she said. "*Background Monthly* sent me out to do a story on the dolphins. Do you work with them?"

"Yes," Mal said. "I started with Dr. Knight in the beginning."

"Oh, good," she said. "Then you can tell me some things. You were here when Dr. Brayt took charge after Dr. Knight's death?"

"Mr. Brayt," he corrected automatically. "Yes." The emotion she moved in him was so deep and strong it seemed she must feel it too. But she gave no sign.

"Mr. Brayt?" she echoed. "Oh. How did the staff take to him?"

"Well," said Mal, wishing she would smile again, "everyone took to him."

"I see," she said. "He's a good research head?"

"A good administrator," said Mal. "He's not involved in the research end."

"He's not?" She stared at him. "But didn't he replace Dr. Knight, after Dr. Knight's death?"

"Why, yes," said Mal. He made an effort to bring his attention back to the conversation. He had never had a woman affect him like this before. "But just as administrator of the station, here. You see—most of our funds for work here come from the Willernie Foundation. They had faith in Dr. Knight, but when he died . . . well, they wanted someone of their own in charge. None of us mind."

"Willernie Foundation," she said. "I don't know it."

"It was set up by a man named Willernie, in St. Louis,

Missouri," said Mal. "He made his money manufacturing kitchen utensils. When he died he left a trust and set up the Foundation to encourage basic research." Mal smiled. "Don't ask me how he got from kitchen utensils to that. That's not much information for you, is it?"

"It's more than I had a minute ago," she smiled back. "Did you know Corwin Brayt before he came here?"

"No." Mal shook his head. "I don't know many people outside the biological and zoological fields."

"I imagine you know him pretty well now, though, after the six months he's been in charge."

"Well—" Mal hesitated, "I wouldn't say I know him *well*, at all. You see, he's up here in the office all day long and I'm down with Pollux and Castor—the two wild dolphins we've got coming to the station, now. Corwin and I don't see each other much."

"On this small island?"

"I suppose it seems funny—but we're both pretty busy."

"I guess you would be." She smiled again. "Will you take me to him?"

"Him?" Mal awoke suddenly to the fact they were still standing on the terrace. "Oh, yes—it's Corwin you came to see."

"Not just Corwin," she said. "I came to see the whole place."

"Well, I'll take you in to the office. Come along."

He led her across the terrace and in through the front door into the air-conditioned coolness of the interior. Corwin Brayt ran the air-conditioning constantly, as if his own somewhat icy personality demanded the dry, distant coldness of a mountain atmosphere. Mal led Jane Wilson down a short corridor and through another door into a large wide-windowed office. A tall, slim, broad-shouldered man with black hair and a brown, coldly handsome face looked up from a large desk, and got to his feet on seeing Jane.

"Corwin," said Mal. "This is Miss Jane Wilson from *Background Monthly*."

"Yes," said Corwin expressionlessly to Jane, coming

around the desk to them. "I got a wire yesterday you were coming." He did not wait for Jane to offer her hand, but offered his own. Their fingers met.

"I've got to be getting down to Castor and Pollux," said Mal, turning away.

"I'll see you later then," Jane said, looking over at him.

"Why, yes. Maybe—" he said. He went out. As he closed the door of Brayt's office behind him, he paused for a moment in the dim, cool hallway, and shut his eyes. *Don't be a fool*, he told himself, *a girl like that can do a lot better than someone like you. And probably has already.*

He opened his eyes and went back down to the pool behind the station and the non-human world of the dolphins.

When he got there, he found that Castor and Pollux were back. Their pool was an open one, with egress to the open blue waters of the Caribbean. In the first days of the research at Dolphin's Way, the dolphins had been confined in a closed pool like any captured wild animal. It was only later on, when the work at the station had come up against what Knight had called "the environmental barrier," that the notion was conceived of opening the pool to the sea, so that the dolphins they had been working with could leave or stay, as they wished.

They had left—but they had come back. Eventually, they had left for good. But strangely, wild dolphins had come from time to time to take their places, so that there were always dolphins at the station.

Castor and Pollux were the latest pair. They had showed up some four months ago after a single dolphin frequenting the station had disappeared. Free, independent— they had been most co-operative. But the barrier had not been breached.

Now, they were sliding back and forth past each other underwater utilizing the full thirty-yard length of the pool, passing beside, over and under each other, their seven-foot nearly identical bodies almost, but not quite, rubbing as they passed. The tape showed them to be talking together up in the supersonic range, eighty to a hundred and twenty kilocycles per second. Their pattern of movement in the water now was something he had never seen before. It was regular and ritualistic as a dance.

He sat down and put on the earphones connected to the hydrophones, underwater at each end of the pool. He spoke into the microphone, asking them about their movements, but they ignored him and kept on with the patterned swimming.

The sound of footsteps behind him made him turn. He saw Jane Wilson approaching down the concrete steps from the back door of the station, with the stocky, overalled figure of Pete Adant, the station mechanic.

"Here he is," said Pete, as they came up. "I've got to get back now."

"Thank you." She gave Pete the smile that had so moved Mal earlier. Pete turned and went back up the steps. She turned to Mal. "Am I interrupting something?"

"No." He took off the earphones. "I wasn't getting any answers, anyway."

She looked at the two dolphins in their underwater dance with the liquid surface swirling above them as they turned now this way, now that, just under it.

"Answers?" she said. He smiled a little ruefully.

"We call them answers," he said. He nodded at the two smoothly streamlined shapes turning in the pool. "Sometimes we ask questions and get responses."

"Informative responses?" she asked.

"Sometimes. You wanted to see me about something?"

"About everything," she said. "It seems you're the man I came to talk to—not Brayt. He sent me down here. I understand you're the one with the theory."

"Theory?" he said warily, feeling his heart sink inside him.

"The notion, then," she said. "The idea that, if there is some sort of interstellar civilization, it might be waiting for the people of Earth to qualify themselves before making contact. And that test might not be a technological one like developing a faster-than-light means of travel, but a sociological one—"

"Like learning to communicate with an alien culture—

a culture like that of the dolphins," he interrupted harshly
"Corwin told you this?"

"I'd heard about it before I came," she said. "I'
thought it was Brayt's theory, though."

"No," said Mal, "it's mine." He looked at her. "Yo
aren't laughing."

"Should I laugh?" she said. She was attentively watch
ing the dolphins' movements. Suddenly he felt sharp jea
ousy toward them for holding her attention; and the emo
tion pricked him to something he might not otherwise hav
had the courage to do.

"Fly over to the mainland with me," he said, "and hav
lunch. I'll tell you all about it."

"All right." She looked up from the dolphins at him a
last and he was surprised to see her frowning. "There's a lo
I don't understand," she murmured. "I thought it was Bray
I had to learn about. But it's you—and the dolphins."

"Maybe we can clear that up at lunch, too," Mal said
not quite clear what she meant, but not greatly caring, ei
ther. "Come on, the helicopters are around the north side o
the building."

They flew a copter across to Carupano, and sat down to
lunch looking out at the shipping in the open roadstead o
the azure sea before the town, while the polite Spanish o
Venezuelan voices sounded from the tables around them.

"Why should I laugh at your theory?" she said again,
when they were settled, and eating lunch.

"Most people take it to be a crackpot excuse for our fail
ure at the station," he said.

Her brown arched brows rose. "Failure?" she said. "I
thought you were making steady progress."

"Yes. And no," he said. "Even before Dr. Knight died,
we ran into something he called the environmental barrier."

"Environmental barrier?"

"Yes." Mal poked with his fork at the shrimp in his sea
food cocktail. "This work of ours all grew out of the work
done by Dr. John Lilly. You read his book, *Man and Dolphin*?"

"No," she said. He looked at her, surprised.

"He was the pioneer in this research with dolphins," Mal said. "I'd have thought reading his book would have been the first thing you would have done before coming down here."

"The first thing I did," she said, "was try to find out something about Corwin Brayt. And I was pretty unsuccessful at that. That's why I landed here with the notion that it was he, not you, who was the real worker with the dolphins."

"That's why you asked me if I knew much about him?"

"That's right," she answered. "But tell me about this environmental barrier."

"There's not a great deal to tell," he said. "Like most big problems, it's simple enough to state. At first, in working with the dolphins, it seemed the early researchers were going great guns, and communication was just around the corner—a matter of interpreting the sounds they made to each other, in the humanly audible range, and above it; and teaching the dolphins human speech."

"It turned out those things couldn't be done?"

"They could. They were done—or as nearly so as makes no difference. But then we came up against the fact that communication doesn't mean understanding." He looked at her. "You and I talk the same language, but do we really understand perfectly what the other person means when he speaks to us?"

She looked at him for a moment, and then slowly shook her head without taking her eyes off his face.

"Well," said Mal, "that's essentially our problem with the dolphins—only on a much larger scale. Dolphins, like Castor and Pollux, can talk with me, and I with them, but we can't understand each other to any great degree."

"You mean intellectually understood, don't you?" Jane said. "Not just mechanically?"

"That's right," Mal answered. "We agree on denotation of an auditory or other symbol, but not on connotation. I can say to Castor—'the Gulf Stream is a strong ocean current' and he'll agree exactly. But neither of us really has the slightest idea of what the other really means. My mental image of the Gulf Stream is not Castor's image. My notion of 'powerful' is relative to the fact I'm six feet tall, weigh a hundred and seventy-five pounds and can lift my own weight against the force of gravity. Castor's is relative to the fact that he is seven feet long, can speed up to forty miles an hour through the water, and as far as he knows weighs nothing, since his four hundred pounds of body-weight are balanced out by the equal weight of the water he displaces. And the concept of lifting something is all but unknown to him. My mental abstraction of 'ocean' is not his, and our ideas of what a current is may coincide, or be literally worlds apart in meaning. And so far we've found no way of bridging the gap between us."

"The dolphins have been trying as well as you?"

"I believe so," said Mal. "But I can't prove it. Any more than I can really prove the dolphin's intelligence to hardcore skeptics until I can come up with something previously outside human knowledge that the dolphins have taught me. Or have them demonstrate that they've learned the use of some human intellectual process. And in these things we've all failed—because, as I believe and Dr. Knight believed, of the connotative gap, which is a result of the environmental barrier."

She sat watching him. He was probably a fool to tell her all this, but he had had no one to talk to like this since Dr. Knight's heart attack, eight months before, and he felt words threatening to pour out of him.

"We've got to learn to think like the dolphins," he said, "or the dolphins have to learn to think like us. For nearly six years now we've been trying and neither side's succeeded." Almost before he thought, he added the one thing he had been determined to keep to himself. "I've been afraid our research funds will be cut off any day now."

"Cut off? By the Willernie Foundation?" she said. "Why would they do that?"

"Because we haven't made any progress for so long," Ial said bitterly. "Or, at least, no provable progress. I'm fraid time's just about run out. And if it runs out, it may ever be picked up again. Six years ago, there was a lot of opular interest in the dolphins. Now, they've been disounted and forgotten, shelved as merely bright animals."

"You can't be sure the research won't be picked up gain."

"But I feel it," he said. "It's part of my notion about the bility to communicate with an alien race being the test for s humans. I feel we've got this one chance and if we flub it, ve'll never have another." He pounded the table softly with is fist. "The worst of it is, I *know* the dolphins are trying ust as hard to get through from their side—if I could only ecognize what they're doing, how they're trying to make ne understand!"

Jane had been sitting watching him.

"You seem pretty sure of that," she said. "What makes ou so sure?"

He unclenched his fist and forced himself to sit back in is chair.

"Have you ever looked into the jaws of a dolphin?" he aid. "They're this long." He spread his hands apart in the ir to illustrate. "And each pair of jaws contains eighty-eight harp teeth. Moreover, a dolphin like Castor weighs several undred pounds and can move at water speeds that are almost incredible to a human. He could crush you easily by amming you against the side of a tank, if he didn't want to ear you apart with his teeth, or break your bones with lows of his flukes." He looked at her grimly. "In spite of all his, in spite of the fact that men have caught and killed dolohins—even we killed them in our early, fumbling reearches, and dolphins are quite capable of using their teeth ind strength on marine enemies—no dolphin has ever been cnown to attack a human being. Aristotle, writing in the ourth Century B.C., speaks of the, quote, gentle and kindy, end quote, nature of the dolphin."

He stopped, and looked at Jane sharply.

"You don't believe me," he said.

"Yes," she said. "Yes, I do." He took a deep breath.

"I'm sorry," he said. "I've made the mistake of mention
ing all this before to other people and been sorry I did. I told
this to one man who gave me his opinion that it indicated
that the dolphin instinctively recognized human superiority
and the value of human life." Mal grinned at her, harshly
"But it was just an instinct. '*Like dogs*,' he said. '*Dogs instinc
tively admire and love people*—' and he wanted to tell me about
a dachshund he'd had, named Poochie, who could read the
morning newspaper and wouldn't bring it in to him if there
was a tragedy reported on the front page. He could prove
this, and Poochie's intelligence, by the number of times he'd
had to get the paper off the front step himself."

Jane laughed. It was a low, happy laugh; and it took the
bitterness suddenly out of Mal.

"Anyway," said Mal, "the dolphin's restraint with hu
mans is just one of the indications, like the wild dolphins
coming to us here at the station, that've convinced me the
dolphins are trying to understand us, too. And have been
maybe, for centuries."

"I don't see why you worry about the research stopping," she said. "With all you know, can't you convince people—"

"There's only one person I've got to convince," said
Mal. "And that's Corwin Brayt. And I don't think I'm doing
it. It's just a feeling—but I feel as if he's sitting in judgment
upon me, and the work. I feel . . ." Mal hesitated, "almost as
if he's a hatchet man."

"He isn't," Jane said. "He can't be. I'll find out for you,
if you like. There're ways of doing it. I'd have the answer
for you right now, if I'd thought of him as an administrator.
But I thought of him as a scientist, and I looked him up in
the wrong places."

Mal frowned at her unbelievingly.

"You don't actually mean you can find out that for
me?" he asked.

She smiled.

"Wait and see," she replied. "I'd like to know, myself, hat his background is."

"It could be important," he said, eagerly. "I know it ounds fantastic—but if I'm right, the research with the dolhins could be important, more important than anything se in the world."

She stood up suddenly from the table.

"I'll go and start checking up right now," she said. Why don't you go on back to the island? It'll take me a few ours and I'll take the water-taxi over."

"But you haven't finished lunch yet," he said. "In fact ou haven't even started lunch. Let's eat first, then you can o."

"I want to call some people and catch them while hey're still at work," she said. "It's the time difference on hese long-distance calls. I'm sorry. We'll have dinner toether, will that do?"

"It'll have to," he said. She melted his disappointment vith one of her amazing smiles, and went.

With her gone, Mal found he was not hungry himself. Ie got hold of the waiter and managed to cancel the main ourse of their meals. He sat and had two more drinks—not omething usual for him. Then he left and flew the copter )ack to the island.

Pete Adant encountered him as he was on his way from he copter park to the dolphin pool.

"There you are," said Pete. "Corwin wants to see you n an hour—when he gets back, that is. He's gone over to he mainland himself."

Ordinarily, such a piece of news would have awakened he foreboding about cancellation of the research that rode ilways like a small, cold, metal weight inside Mal. But the total of three drinks and no lunch had anesthetized him somewhat. He nodded and went on to the pool.

The dolphins were still there, still at their patterned swimming. Or was he just imagining the pattern? Mal sat down on his chair by the poolside before the tape recorder

which set down a visual pattern of the sounds made by th
dolphins. He put the earphones to the hydrophones or
switching on the mike before him.

Suddenly, it struck him how futile all this was. He ha
gone through these same motions daily for four years now
And what was the sum total of results he had to show for it
Reel on reel of tape recording a failure to hold any trul
productive conversation with the dolphins.

He took the earphones off and laid them aside. He lit
cigarette and sat gazing with half-seeing eyes at the under
water ballet of the dolphins. To call it ballet was almost t
libel their actions. The gracefulness, the purposefulness o
their movements, buoyed up by the salt water, was beyon
that of any human in air or on land. He thought again o
what he had told Jane Wilson about the dolphins' refusal t
attack their human captors, even when the humans hurt o
killed them. He thought of the now-established fact that dol
phins will come to the rescue of one of their own who ha
been hurt or knocked unconscious, and hold him up on top
of the water so he will not drown—the dolphin's breathing
process requiring conscious control, so that it fails if the dol
phin becomes unconscious.

He thought of their playfulness, their affection, the
wide and complex range of their speech. In any of those cat
egories, the average human stacked up beside them looked
pretty poor. In the dolphin culture there was no visible im
pulse to war, to murder, to hatred and unkindness. No won
der, thought Mal, they and we have trouble understanding
each other. In a different environment, under different
conditions, they're the kind of people we've always strug
gled to be. We have the technology, the tool-using capabili
ty, but with it all in many ways we're more animal than
they are.

Who's to judge which of us is better, he thought, look
ing at their movements through the water with the sligh
hazy melancholy induced by the three drinks on an empty
stomach. I might be happier myself, if I were a dolphin. For
a second, the idea seemed deeply attractive. The endless
open sea, the freedom, an end to all the complex structure o

uman culture on land. A few lines of poetry came back to
im.

"*Come Children,*" he quoted out loud to himself, "*let us
way! Down and away, below . . .!*"

He saw the two dolphins pause in their underwater bal-
t and saw that the microphone before him was on. Their
eads turned toward the microphone underwater at the
ear end of the pool. He remembered the following lines,
nd he quoted them aloud to the dolphins.

> . . . *Now my brothers call from the bay,*
> *Now the great winds shoreward blow,*
> *Now the salt tides seaward flow;*
> *Now the wild white horses play,*
> *Champ and chafe and toss in the spray—**

He broke off suddenly, feeling self-conscious. He
oked down at the dolphins. For a moment they merely
ung where they were under the surface, facing the micro-
hone. Then Castor turned and surfaced. His forehead with
ts blowhole broke out into the air and then his head as he
oked up at Mal. His airborne voice from the blowhole's
ensitive lips and muscles spoke quacking words at the hu-
nan.

"*Come, Mal,*" he quacked, "*Let us away! Down and away!
Below!*"

The head of Pollux surfaced beside Castor's. Mal stared
t them for a long second. Then he jerked his gaze back to
he tape of the recorder. There on it, was the rhythmic re-
ord of his own voice as it had sounded in the pool, and be-
ow it on their separate tracks, the tapes showed parallel
hythms coming from the dolphins. They had been match-
ng his speech largely in the inaudible range while he was
quoting.

Still staring, Mal got to his feet, his mind trembling
with a suspicion so great he hesitated to put it into words.
Like a man in a daze he walked to the near end of the pool,

*"*The Forsaken Merman,*" by Matthew Arnold, 1849.

where three steps led down into the shallower part. Here
the water was only three feet deep.

"*Come, Mal!*" quacked Castor, as the two still hung in
the water with their heads out, facing him. "*Let us away!
Down and away! Below!*"

Step by step, Mal went down into the pool. He felt the
coolness of the water wetting his pants legs, rising to his
waist as he stood at last on the pool floor. A few feet in front
of him, the two dolphins hung in the water, facing him,
waiting. Standing with the water rippling lightly above his
belt buckle, Mal looked at them, waiting for some sign, some
signal of what they wanted him to do.

They gave him no clue. They only waited. It was up to
him to go forward on his own. He sloshed forward into
deeper water, put his head down, held his breath and
pushed himself off underwater.

In the forefront of his blurred vision, he saw the grainy
concrete floor of the pool. He glided slowly over it, rising a
little, and suddenly the two dolphins were all about him—
gliding over, above, around his own underwater floating
body, brushing lightly against him as they passed, making
him a part of their underwater dance. He heard the creaking
that was one of the underwater sounds they made and knew
that they were probably talking in ranges he could not hear.
He could not know what they were saying, he could not
sense the meaning of their movements about him, but the
feeling that they were trying to convey information to him
was inescapable.

He began to feel the need to breathe. He held out as
long as he could, then let himself rise to the surface. He
broke water and gulped air, and the two dolphin heads
popped up nearby, watching him. He dived under the surface again. *I am a dolphin*—he told himself almost desperately—*I am not a man, but a dolphin, and to me all this means—
what?*

Several times he dived, and each time the persistent and
disciplined movements of the dolphins about him underwater convinced him more strongly that he was on the right

ack. He came up, blowing, at last. He was not carrying the
tempt to be like them far enough, he thought. He turned
nd swam back to the steps at the shallow end of the pool,
nd began to climb out.

"*Come, Mal—let us away!*" quacked a dolphin voice be-
ind him, and he turned to see the heads of both Castor and
ollux out of the water, regarding him with mouths open
rgently.

"Come Children—down and away!" he repeated, as re-
ssuringly as he could intonate the words.

He hurried up to the big cabinet of the supply locker at
he near end of the pool, and opened the door of the section
f skin-diving equipment. He needed to make himself more
ke a dolphin. He considered the air tanks and the mask of
he scuba equipment, and rejected them. The dolphins could
ot breathe underwater any more than he could. He started
erking things out of the cabinet.

A minute or so later he returned to the steps in swim-
ning trunks, wearing a glass mask with a snorkel tube, and
wim fins on his feet. In his hand he carried two lengths of
oft rope. He sat down on the steps and with the rope tied
is knees and ankles together. Then, clumsily, he hopped
nd splashed into the water.

Lying face down in the pool, staring at the bottom
hrough his glass faceplate, he tried to move his bound legs
ogether like the flukes of a dolphin, to drive himself slant-
ngly down under the surface.

After a moment or two he managed it. In a moment the
dolphins were all about him as he tried to swim underwater,
dolphinwise. After a little while his air ran short again and
he had to surface. But he came up like a dolphin and lay on
he surface filling his lungs, before fanning himself down
flukefashion with his swim fins. *Think like a dolphin*, he kept
repeating to himself over and over. *I am a dolphin. And this is
my world. This is the way it is.*

. . . And Castor and Pollux were all about him.

The sun was setting in the far distance of the ocean
when at last he dragged himself, exhausted, up the steps of

the pool and sat down on the poolside. To his water-soaked
body, the twilight breeze felt icy. He unbound his legs, took
off his fins and mask and walked wearily to the cabinet.
From the nearest compartment he took a towel and dried
himself, then put on an old bathrobe he kept hanging there.
He sat down in an aluminum deckchair beside the cabinet
and sighed with weariness.

He looked out at the red sun dipping its lower edge in
the sea, and felt a great warm sensation of achievement inside him. In the darkening pool, the two dolphins still swam
back and forth. He watched the sun descending . . .

"Mal!"

The sound of Corwin Brayt's voice brought his head
around. When he saw the tall, cold-faced man was coming
toward him with the slim figure of Jane alongside, Mal got
up quickly from his chair. They came up to him.

"Why didn't you come in to see me as I asked?" Brayt
said. "I left word for you with Pete. I didn't even know you
were back from the mainland until the water-taxi brought
Miss Wilson out just now, and she told me."

"I'm sorry," said Mal. "I think I've run into something
here—"

"Never mind telling me now." Brayt's voice was hurried and sharpened with annoyance. "I had a good deal to
speak to you about, but there's not time now if I'm to catch
the mainland plane to St. Louis. I'm sorry to break it this
way—" He checked himself and turned to Jane. "Would you
excuse us, Miss Wilson? Private business. If you'll give us a
second—"

"Of course," she said. She turned and walked away
from them alongside the pool, into the deepening twilight.
The dolphins paced her in the water. The sun was just
down now, and with the sudden oncoming of tropical night,
stars could be seen overhead.

"Just let me tell you," said Mal. "It's about the research."

"I'm sorry," said Brayt. "There's no point in your telling me now. I'll be gone a week and I want you to watch out

r this Jane Wilson, here." He lowered his voice slightly. "I
lked to *Background Monthly* on the phone this afternoon,
id the editor I spoke to there didn't know about the article,
recognize her name—"

"Somebody new," said Mal. "Probably someone who
idn't know her."

"At any rate it makes no difference," said Brayt. "As I
y, I'm sorry to tell you in such a rushed fashion, but Wil-
rnie has decided to end its grant of funds to the station.
m flying to St. Louis to settle details." He hesitated. "I'm
ire you knew something like this was coming, Mal." Mal
ared, shocked.

"It was inevitable," said Brayt coldly. "You knew that."
Ie paused. "I'm sorry."

"But the station'll fold without the Willernie support!"
iid Mal, finding his voice. "You know that. And just today
found out what the answer is! Just this afternoon! Listen to
ie!" He caught Brayt's arm as the other started to turn
way. "The dolphins have been trying to contact us. Oh, not
t first, not when we experimented with captured speci-
iens. But since we opened the pool to the sea. The only
:ouble was we insisted on trying to communicate by sound
lone—and that's all but impossible for them."

"Excuse me," said Brayt, trying to disengage his arm.

"Listen, will you!" said Mal, desperately. "Their com-
iunication process is an incredibly rich one. It's as if you
nd I communicated by using all the instruments in a sym-
ihony orchestra. They not only use sound from four to a
undred and fifty kilocycles per second, they use move-
nent, and touch—and all of it in reference to the ocean con-
iitions surrounding them at the moment."

"I've got to go."

"Just a minute. Don't you remember what Lilly hy-
iothesized about the dolphins' methods of navigation? He
uggested that it was a multivariable method, using tem-
ierature, speed, taste of the water, position of the stars, sun
nd so forth, all fed into their brains simultaneously and in-
tantaneously. Obviously, it's true, and obviously their pro-

cess of communication is also a multivariable method utilizing sound, touch, position, place and movement. Now that we know this, we can go into the sea with them and try to operate across their whole spectrum of communication. No wonder we weren't able to get across anything but the most primitive exchanges, restricting ourselves to sound. It's been equivalent to restricting human communication to just the nouns in each sentence, while maintaining the sentence structure—"

"I'm very sorry!" said Brayt, firmly. "I tell you, Mal. None of this makes any difference. The decision of the Foundation is based on financial reasons. They've got just so much money available to donate, and this station's allotment has already gone in other directions. There's nothing that can be done now."

He pulled his arm free.

"I'm sorry," he said again. "I'll be back in a week at the outside. You might be thinking of how to wind up things here."

He turned with that, and went away, around the building toward the parking spot of the station copters. Mal, stunned, watched the tall, slim, broad-shouldered figure move off into darkness.

"It doesn't matter," said the gentle voice of Jane comfortingly at his ear. He jerked about and saw her facing him. "You won't need the Willernie funds any more."

"He told you?" Mal stared at her as she shook her head, smiling in the growing dimness. "You heard? From way over there?"

"Yes," she said. "And you were right about Brayt. I got your answer for you. He was a hatchet man—sent here by the Willernie people to decide whether the station deserved further funds."

"But we've got to have them!" Mal said. "It won't take much more, but we've got to go into the sea and work out ways to talk to the dolphins in their own mode. We've got to expand to their level of communication, not try to compress

1em to ours. You see, this afternoon, I had a break-
1rough—"

"I know," she said. "I know all about it."

"You know?" He stared at her. "How do you know?"

"You've been under observation all afternoon," she
1id. "You're right. You did break through the environmen-
1l barrier. From now on it's just a matter of working out
1ethods."

"Under observation? How?" Abruptly, that seemed the
1ast important thing at hand. "But I have to have money,"
1e said. "It'll take time and equipment, and that costs mon-
y—"

"No." Her voice was infinitely gentle. "You won't need
o work out your own methods. Your work is done, Mal.
'his afternoon the dolphins and you broke the bars to com-
1unication between the two races for the first time in the
1istory of either. It was the job you set out to do and you
1ere part of it. You can be happy knowing that."

"Happy?" He almost shouted at her, suddenly. "I don't
1nderstand what you're talking about."

"I'm sorry." There was a ghost of a sigh from her.
'We'll show you how to talk to the dolphins, Mal, if men
1eed to. As well as some other things—perhaps." Her face
ifted to him under the star-marked sky, still a little light in
he west. "You see, you were right about something more
han dolphins, Mal. Your idea that the ability to communi-
ate with another intelligent race, an alien race, was a test
hat had to be passed before the superior species of a planet
ould be contacted by the intelligent races of the galaxy—
hat was right, too."

He stared at her. She was so close to him, he could feel
he living warmth of her body, although they were not
ouching. He saw her, he felt her, standing before him; and
1e felt all the strange deep upwelling of emotion that she
1ad released in him the moment he first saw her. The deep
1motion he felt for her still. Suddenly understanding came
o him.

"You mean you're not from Earth—" his voice wa hoarse and uncertain. It wavered to a stop. "But you're hu man!" he cried desperately.

She looked back at him a moment before answering. I the dimness he could not tell for sure, but he thought he saw the glisten of tears in her eyes.

"Yes," she said, at last, slowly. "In the way you mea that—you can say I'm human."

A great and almost terrible joy burst suddenly in him It was the joy of a man who, in the moment when he think he has lost everything, finds something of infinitely greate value.

"But how?" he said, excitedly, a little breathlessly. H pointed up at the stars. "If you come from some place—u there? How can you be human?"

She looked down, away from his face.

"I'm sorry," she said. "I can't tell you."

"Can't tell me? Oh," he said with a little laugh, "yo mean I wouldn't understand."

"No—" Her voice was almost inaudible, "I mean I'n not allowed to tell you."

"Not allowed—" he felt an unreasoning chill about hi heart. "But Jane—" He broke off fumbling for words. " don't know quite how to say this, but it's important to me to know. From the first moment I saw you there, I ... I mean maybe you don't feel anything like this, you don't know what I'm talking about—"

"Yes," she whispered. "I do."

"Then—" he stared at her. "You could at least say something that would set my mind at rest. I mean ... it's only a matter of time now. We're going to be getting togeth er, your people and I, aren't we?"

She looked up at him out of darkness.

"No," she said, "we aren't, Mal. Ever. And that's why I can't tell you anything."

"We aren't?" he cried. "We aren't? But you came and saw us communicate— Why aren't we?"

She looked up at him for the last time, then, and told him. He, having heard what she had to say, stood still; still as a stone, for there was nothing left to do. And she, turning slowly and finally away from him, went off to the edge of the pool and down the steps into the shallow water, where the dolphins came rushing to meet her, their foamy tearing of the surface making a wake as white as snow.

Then the three of them moved, as if by magic, across the surface of the pool and out the entrance of it to the ocean. And so they continued to move off until they were lost to sight in darkness and the starlit, glinting surface of the waves.

It came to Mal then, as he stood there, that the dolphins must have been waiting for her all this time. All the wild dolphins, who had come to the station after the first two captives, were set free to leave or stay as they wanted. The dolphins had known, perhaps for centuries, that it was to them alone on Earth that the long-awaited visitors from the stars would finally come.

# Pithecanthropus Rejectus

## by Manly Wade Wellman

My first memories seem to be those of the normal human child—nursery, toys, adults seriously making meaningless observations with charts, tape measures and scales. Well, rather more than average of that last item, the observations. My constant companion was a fat, blue-eyed baby that drooled and gurgled and barely crept upon the nursery linoleum, while I scurried easily hither and thither, scrambling up on tables and bedposts, and sometimes on the bureau. I felt sorry for him now and then. But he was amazingly happy and healthy, and gave no evidence of having the sudden fearful pains that struck me in head and jaw from time to time.

As I learned to speak and to comprehend, I found out the cause of those pains. I was told by the tall, smiling blonde woman who taught me to call her "Mother." She explained that I had been born with no opening in the top of my skull—so needed for bone and brain expression—and

that the man of the house—"Doctor"—had made such an
opening, governing the growth of my cranium and later
stopping the hole with a silver plate. My jaw, too, had been
altered with silver, for when I was born it had been too shallow and narrow to give my tongue play. The building of a
chin for me and the remodeling of several tongue-muscles
had made it possible for me to speak. I learned before the
baby did, by several months. I learned to say Mother, Doctor, to call the baby "Sidney" and myself "Congo." Later I
could make my wants known although, as this writing
shows and will show, I was never fluent.

Doctor used to come into the nursery and make notes
by the hour, watching my every move and pricking up his
ears at my every sound. He was a stout, high-shouldered
man, with a strong, square beard. He acted grave—almost
stern—where I was involved. But with baby Sidney he
played most tenderly. I used to feel hurt and would go to
Mother for sympathy. She had enough for me and Sidney,
too. She would pick me up and cuddle me and laugh—give
me her cheek to kiss.

Once or twice Doctor scowled, and once I overheard
him talking to Mother just beyond the nursery door. I understood pretty well even then, and since that time I have
filled in details of the conversation.

"I tell you, I don't like it," he snapped. "Showering at-
tentions on that creature."

She gave him a ready laugh. "Poor little Congo!"

"Congo's an ape, for all my surgery," he replied coldly.
"Sidney is your son, and Sidney alone. The other is an experiment—like a shake-up of chemicals in a tube, or a graft-
ing of twigs on a tree."

"Let me remind you," said Mother, still good-natured,
"that when you brought him from the zoo, you said he must
live here as a human child, on equal terms with Sidney.
That, remember, was part of the experiment. And so are affection and companionship."

"Ah, the little beast!" Doctor almost snarled. "Sometimes I wish I hadn't begun these observations."

"But you have. You increased his brain powers and made it possible for him to speak. He's brighter than any human child his age."

"Apes mature quickly. He'll come to the peak of development and Sidney will forge ahead. That always happens in these experiments."

"These experiments have always been performed with ordinary ape-children before," said Mother. "With your operations you've given him something, at least, of human character. So give him something of human consideration as well."

"I'm like Prospero, going out of my way to lift up Caliban from the brute."

"Caliban meant well," Mother responded, reminding him of something I knew nothing about. "Meanwhile, I don't do things by halves, dear. As long as Congo remains in this house, he shall have kindness and help from me. And he shall look to me as his mother."

I heard and, in time, digested all of this. When I learned to read, during my third year, I got hold of some of Doctor's published articles about me and began to realize what everything meant.

Of course, I'd seen myself in mirrors hundreds of times and knew that I was dark, bow-legged and long-armed, with a face that grew out at an acute angle, and hair all over my body. Yet this had not set me very far apart, in my own mind, from the others. I was different from Sidney—but so was Doctor and so was Mother, in appearance, size and behavior. I was closer to them—in speech and such things as table manners and self-reliance—than he. But now I learned and grew to appreciate the difference between me, on one side, and Sidney, Doctor and Mother on the other.

I had been born, I found, in an iron cage at the Bronx Zoo. My mother was a great ape, a Kulakamba, very close to human type in body, size and intelligence—not dwarfed like a common chimpanzee nor thickset and surly like a gorilla. Doctor, a great experimental anthropologist—words like those happen to be easy for me, since they were part of daily

talk at Doctor's house—had decided to make observations on
a baby ape and his own newborn child, rearing them side by
side under identical conditions. I was the baby ape.

Incidentally, I have read in a book called "Trader
Horn" that there are no Kulakambas, that they are only a
fairy story. But there are—many and many of us, in the
Central African forests.

I tell these things very glibly, as if I knew all about
them. Doctor had written reams about the Kulakamba, and
clippings of all he wrote were kept in the library. I had re-
course to them as I grew older.

When I was four, Doctor led me into his big white laboratory. There he examined and measured my hands, grunt-
ing perplexedly into his beard.

"We'll have to operate," he said at last.

"Will we?" I quavered. I knew what the word meant.

He smiled, but not exactly cheerfully. "You'll have an
anesthetic," he promised, as though it were a great favor. "I
want to fix your hands. The thumbs don't oppose and it
makes your grasp clumsy. Not human, Congo; not human."

I was frightened, but Mother came to comfort me and
say that I would be better off in the long run. So, when Doctor commanded, I lay on the sheet-spread table and breathed
hard into the cloth he put on my face. I went to sleep and
dreamed of high, green trees and of people like myself, who
climbed and played there—building nests and eating nuts as
big as my head. In my dream I tried to join them, but found
myself held back, as if by a pane of glass. That made me
shed tears—though some say that apes cannot shed tears—
and thus weeping, I awoke. My hands had a dull soreness in
them and were swathed in bandages to the elbows. After
weeks, I could use them again and found that their calloused
palms had been softened, the awkward little thumbs somehow lengthened and newly jointed. I grew so skillful with
them that I could pick up a pin or tie a bow knot. This was
in the winter time, and once or twice when I played on the
porch I had terrible pains in brow and jaw. Doctor said that
the cold made my silver plates hurt, and that I must never
go outside without a warm cap and a muffler wrapped high.

"It's like a filling against a nerve of a tooth," he explained.

At seven I was all about the house, helping Mother very deftly with her work. Now Doctor grew enthusiastic about me. He would lecture us all at the table—Sidney and I ate with him when there was no company—and said that his experiment, faulty in some ways, gave promise of great things along an unforeseen line.

"Congo was only a normal ape-cub," he would insist, "and he's developing in every possible way into a very respectable lower-class human being."

"He's by no means lower-class," Mother always argued at this point, but Doctor would plunge ahead.

"We could operate on his people wholesale, make wonderful, cheap labor available. Why, when Congo grows up he'll be as strong as six or eight men, and his keep is almost nothing."

He tested me at various occupations—gardening, carpentry and ironworking, at which last I seem to have done quite well—and one day he asked me what I would rather do than anything else.

I remembered the dream I had had when he operated on me—and many times since. "Best of all," I replied, "I would like to live in a tree, build a nest of leaves and branches—"

"Ugh!" he almost screamed in disgust. "And I thought you were becoming human!"

After that he renewed his demands that Mother treat me with less affection.

Sidney was going to school at this time. I remained at home with Doctor and Mother—we lived in a small New Jersey town—and confined most of my activities to the house and the shrub-grown back yard. Once I ran away, after a little quarrel with Doctor, and frightened the entire neighborhood before I was brought back by a nervous policeman with a drawn revolver. Doctor punished me by confining me to my room for three days. During that lonely time I did a lot of thinking and set myself down as an outcast. I had been considered strange, fearful and altogether unbelonging, by human beings. My crooked body and hairy skin had betrayed me to enmity and capture.

At the age of ten I gained my full growth. I was five feet six inches tall and weighed as much as Doctor. My face, once pallid, had become quite black, with bearded jaws and bristly hair on the upper lip. I walked upright, without touching my knuckles to the ground as ordinary apes do, for I usually held some tool or book in my hands. By listening to Sidney as he studied aloud at night I got some smattering of schooling, and built upon this by constant and serious reading of his discarded textbooks. I have been told that the average shut-in child is apt to do the same. On top of this, I read a great deal in Doctor's library, especially travel. But I disliked fiction.

"Why should I read it?" I asked Mother when she offered me a book about "Tom Sawyer." "It isn't true."

"It's interesting," she said.

"But if it's not true, it's a lie; and a lie is wicked."

She pointed out that novel-readers knew all the time that the books were not true. To that I made answer that novel-readers were fools. Doctor, joining the conversation, asked me why, then, I enjoyed my dreams.

"You say that you dream of great green forests," he reminded. "That's no more true than the books."

"If it is a good dream," I replied, "I am glad when I wake, because it made me happy. If it is a bad dream, I am glad because I escape by waking. Anyway, dreams happen and novels do not."

Doctor called it a *sophistication*, and let that conclude the argument.

I have said that I am no proper writer, and I have shown it by overlooking an important fact—the many visits of scientists. They came to observe and to discuss things with Doctor, and even with me. But one day some men appeared who were not scientists. They smoked long cigars and wore diamond rings and derby hats. Doctor had them in his study for an hour, and that night he talked long to Mother.

"One hundred thousand dollars!" he kept saying. "Think of it!"

"You've never thought of money before," she said sadly.

"But a hundred th—my dear, it would be only the beginning. We'd do the experiment again with two baby apes—two new little Congos for you to fuss over—"

"And the first Congo, my poor jungle foster son," mourned Mother. "He'd be miserable somewhere. How can you think of such a thing, dear? Didn't your grandfather fight to free slaves in his day?"

"Those were human slaves," replied Doctor. "Not animals. And Congo won't be miserable. His ape-instinct will enjoy the new life. It'll fairly glitter for him. And we need the money to live on and to experiment with."

That went on and on, and Mother cried. But Doctor had his way. In the morning the men with the cigars came back, and Doctor greeted them gayly. They gave him a check—a big one, for they wrote it very reverently. Then he called me.

"Congo," he said, "you're to go with these people. You've got a career now, my boy; you're in the show business."

I did not want to go, but I had to.

My adventures as a theatrical curiosity have been described in many newspapers all over the world, and I will mention them but briefly. First I was rehearsed to do feats of strength and finish the act with alleged comedy—a dialogue between myself and a man in clown costume. After that, a more successful turn was evolved for me, wherein I was on the stage alone. I performed on a trapeze and a bicycle, then told my life story and answered questions asked by the audiences. I worked in a motion picture, too, with a former swimming champion. I liked him on sight, as much as I liked any human being except Mother. He was always kind and understanding, and did not hate me, even when we were given equal billing.

For a while many newspaper reports thought I was a

fake—a man dressed up in a fur suit—but that was easily disproved. A number of scientists came to visit me in the various cities I performed in, and literally millions of curious people. In my third year as a showpiece I went to Europe. I had to learn French and German, or enough to make myself understood on the stage, and got laughed at for my accent, which was not very good. Once or twice I was threatened, because I said something in the theaters about this political leader or that, but for the most part people were very friendly.

Finally, however, I got a bad cough. My owners were fearfully worried and called a doctor, who prescribed a sea voyage. Lots of publicity came of the announcement that I would sail south, to "visit my homeland of Africa."

Of course I had not been born in Africa, but in the Bronx Zoo; yet a thrill came into my heart when, draped in a long coat and leaning on the rail, we sighted the west coast just below the Equator.

That night, as the ship rode at anchor near some little port, I contrived to slip overside and into a barge full of packing cases. I rode with it to land and sneaked out upon the dock, through the shabby little town, and away up a little stream that led into a hot, green forest.

I tell it so briefly and calmly because that is the way the impulse came to me. I read somewhere about the lemmings, the little ratlike animals that go to the sea and drown themselves by the thousands. That is because they must. I doubt if they philosophize about it; they simply do it. Something like that dragged me ashore in Africa and up the watercourse.

I was as strange and awkward there as any human being would be for the first time. But I knew, somehow, that nature would provide the right things. In the morning I rested in a thicket of fruit trees. The fruit I did not know, but the birds had pecked at it, so I knew it was safe for eating. The flavor was strange but good. By the second day I was well beyond civilization. I slept that night in a tree, making a sort of nest there. It was clumsy work, but something beyond my experience seemed to guide my hands.

After more days, I found my people, the Kulakambas.

They were as they had been in the dream, swinging in treetops, playing and gathering food. Some of the younger ones scampered through the branches, shrilling joyfully over their game of tag. They talked, young and old—they had a language, with inflections and words and probably grammar. I could see a little village of nests, in the forks of the big greens; well-made shelters, with roofs over them. Those must have been quickly and easily made. Nothing troubled the Kulakambas. They lived without thought or worry for the next moment. When the next moment came they lived that, too.

I thought I would approach. I would make friends, learn their ways and their speech. Then I might teach them useful things, and in turn they would teach me games. Already the old dream was a reality and the civilization I had known was slipping away—like a garment that had fitted too loosely.

I approached and came into view. They saw, and began to chatter at me. I tried to imitate their sounds, and I failed.

Then they grew excited and climbed along in the trees above me. They began dropping branches and fruits and such things. I ran, and they followed, shrieking in a rage that had come upon them from nowhere and for no reason I could think of. They chased me all that day, until nightfall. A leopard frightened them then, and me as well.

I returned, after many days, to the town by the sea. My owners were there, and greeted me with loud abuse. I had cost them money and worry, important in the order named. One of them wanted to beat me with a whip. I reminded him that I could tear him apart like a roast chicken and there was no more talk of whipping me. I was kept shut up, however, until our ship came back and took us aboard.

Nevertheless, the adventure turned out well, so far as my owners were concerned. Reporters interviewed me when I got back to London. I told them the solemn truth about what I had done, and they made publicity marvels out of the ape-man's return to the jungle.

I made a personal appearance with my picture, for it had come to England just at that time. A week or so later came a cable from America. Somebody was reviving the plays of William Shakespeare, and I was badly wanted for an important role. We sailed back, were interviewed by a battery of reporters on landing, and went to an uptown hotel. Once or twice before there had been trouble about my staying in hotels. Now I was known and publicized as a Shakespearean actor, and the management of the biggest and most sumptuous hotel was glad to have me for a guest.

At once my owners signed a contract for me to appear in "The Tempest." The part given me to study was that of Caliban, a sort of monster who was presented as the uncouth, unwelcome villain. Part of the time he had to be wicked, and part of the time ridiculous. As I read of his fumblings and blunderings, I forgot my long-held dislike of fiction and fable. I remembered what Doctor and Mother had said about Caliban, and all at once I knew how the poor whelp of Sycorax felt.

The next day a visitor came. It was Doctor.

He was grayer than when I had seen him, but healthy and happy and rich-looking. His beard was trimmed to a point instead of square, and he had white edging on his vest. He shook my hand and acted glad to see me.

"You're a real success, Congo," he said over and over again. "I told you that you'd be." We talked a while over this and that, and after a few minutes my owners left the room to do some business or other. Then Doctor leaned forward and patted my knee.

"I say, Congo," he grinned, "how would you like to have some brothers and sisters?"

I did not understand him, and I said so.

"Oh, perfectly simple," he made reply, crossing his legs. "There are going to be more like you."

"More Kulakambas?"

He nodded. "Yes. With brains to think with, and jaws to talk with. You've been a success, I say—profitable, fascinating. And my next experiment will be even better, more accurate. Then others—each a valuable property—each an advance in surgery and psychology over the last."

"Don't do it, Doctor," I said all at once.

"Don't do it?" he repeated sharply. "Why not?"

I tried to think of something compelling to reply, but nothing came to mind. I just said, "Don't do it, Doctor," as I had already.

He studied me a moment, with narrow eyes, then he snorted just as he had in the old days. "You're going to say it's cruel, I suppose," he sneered at me.

"That is right. It is cruel."

"Why, you—" He broke off without calling me anything, but I could feel his scorn, like a hot light upon me: "I suppose you know that if I hadn't done what I did to you, you'd be just a monkey scratching yourself."

I remembered the Kulakambas, happy and thoughtless in the wilderness.

He went on, "I gave you a mind and hands and speech, the three things that make up a man. Now you—"

"Yes," I interrupted again, for I remembered what I had been reading about Caliban. "Speech enough to curse you."

He uncrossed his legs. "A moment ago you were begging me not to do something."

"I'll beg again, Doctor," I pleaded, pushing my anger back into myself. "Don't butcher more beasts into—what I am."

He looked past me, and when he spoke it was not to me, but to himself. "I'll operate on five at first, ten the next year, and maybe get some assistants to do even more. In six or eight years there'll be a full hundred like you, or more advanced—"

"You mustn't," I said very firmly, and leaned forward in my turn.

He jumped up. "You forget yourself, Congo," he growled. "I'm not used to the word 'mustn't'—especially from a thing that owes me so much. And especially when I will lighten the labor of mankind."

"By laying mankind's labor on poor beasts."

"What are you going to do about it?" he flung out.

"I will prevent you," I promised.

He laughed. "You can't. All these gifts of yours mean nothing. You have a flexible tongue, a rational brain—but you're a beast by law and by nature. You can't make a stand of any kind."

"I will prevent you," I said again, and I got up slowly.

He understood then, and yelled loudly. I heard an answering cry in the hall outside. He ran for the door, but I caught him. I remember how easily his neck broke in my hands. Just like a carrot.

The police came and got me, with guns and gas bombs and chains. I was taken to a jail and locked in the strongest cell, with iron bars all around. Outside some police officials and an attorney or two talked.

"He can't be tried for murder," said someone. "He's only an animal, and not subject to human laws."

"He was aware of what he did," argued a policeman. "He's as guilty as the devil."

"But we can hardly bring him into court," replied one of the attorneys. "Why, the newspapers would kid us clear out of the country—out of the legal profession."

They puzzled for a moment, all together. Then one of the police officers slapped his knee. "I've got it," he said, and they all looked at him hopefully.

"Why talk about trials?" demanded the inspired one. "If he can't be tried for killing that medic, neither can we be tried for killing him."

"Not if we do it painlessly," seconded someone.

They saw I was listening, and moved away and talked softly for a full quarter of an hour. Then they all nodded their heads as if agreeing on something. One police captain, fat and white-haired, came to the bars of my cell and looked through.

"Any last thing you'd like to have?" he asked me, not at all unkindly.

I asked for pen and ink and paper, and time enough to write this.

# The Exalted

## by L. Sprague de Camp

The storylike man with the gray goatee shuffled the twelve black billets around on the table top. "Try it again," he said.

The undergraduate sighed "O.K., Professor Methuen. " He looked apprehensively at Johnny Black, sitting across the table with one claw on the button of the stop clock. Johnny returned the look impassively through the spectacles perched on his yellowish muzzle.

"Go," said Ira Methuen.

Johnny depressed the button. The undergraduate started the second of his wiggly-block tests. The twelve billets formed a kind of three-dimensional jigsaw puzzle; when assembled they would make a cube. But the block had originally been sawn apart on wavy, irregular lines, so that the twelve billets had to be put together just so.

The undergraduate fiddled with the billets, trying this one and that one against one he held in his hand. The clock ticked round. In four minutes he had all but one in place.

**131**

This one, a corner piece, simply would not fit. The under-graduate wiggled it and pushed it. He looked at it closely and tried again. But its maladjustment remained.

The undergraduate gave up. "What's the trick?" he asked.

Methuen reversed the billet end for end. It fitted.

"Oh, heck," said the undergraduate. "I could have got it if it hadn't been for Johnny."

Instead of being annoyed, Johnny Black twitched his mouth in a bear's equivalent of a grin. Methuen asked the student why.

"He distracts me somehow. I know he's friendly and all that, but . . . it's this way, sort of. Here I come to Yale to get to be a psychologist. I hear all about testing animals, chimps, and bears, and such. And when I get here I find a bear test-ing *me*. It's kind of upsetting."

"That's all right," said Methuen. "Just what we wanted. We're after not your wiggly-block score by itself, but the ef-fect of Johnny's presence on people taking the test. We're getting Johnny's distraction factor—his ability to distract people. We're also getting the distraction factor of a lot of other things, such as various sounds and smells. I didn't tell you sooner because the knowledge might have affected your performance."

"I see. Do I still get my five bucks?"

"Of course. Good day, Kitchell. Come on, Johnny; we've just got time to make Psychobiology 100. We'll clean up the stuff later."

On the way out of Methuen's office, Johnny asked: "Hey, boss! Do you feer any effec' yet?"

"Not a bit," said Methuen. "I think my original theory was right: that the electrical resistance of the gap between human neurons is already as low as it can be, so the Methu-en injections won't have any appreciable effect on a human being. Sorry, Johnny, but I'm afraid your boss won't be-come any genius as a result of trying a dose of his own medi-cine."

The Methuen treatment had raised Johnny's intelligence from that of a normal black bear to that of—or more exactly to the equivalent of that of—a human being. It had enabled him to carry out those spectacular coups in the Virgin Islands and the Central Park Zoo. It had also worked on a number of other animals in the said zoo, with regrettable results.

Johnny grumbled in his urso-American: "Sir, I don't sink it is smart to teach a crass when you are furr of zat stuff. You never know—"

But they had arrived. The class comprised a handful of grave graduate students, on whom Johnny's distraction factor had little effect.

Ira Methuen was not a good lecturer. He put in too many uh's and er's, and tended to mumble. Besides, Psychobiology 100 was an elementary survey, and Johnny was pretty well up in the field himself. So he settled himself to a view of the Grove Street Cemetery across the street, and to melancholy reflections on the short life span of his species compared with that of men.

"*Ouch!*"

R. H. Wimpus, B.S. '68, jerked his backbone from its normally nonchalant arc into a quivering reflex curve. His eyes were wide with mute indignation.

Methuen was saying: "—whereupon it was discovered that the . . . uh . . . paralysis of the pes resulting from excision of the corresponding motor area of the cortex was much more lasting among the Simiidae than among the other catarrhine primates; that it was more lasting among these than among the platyrrhines—Mr. Wimpus?"

"Nothing," said Wimpus. "I'm sorry."

"And that the platyrrhines, in turn, suffered more than the leuroids and tarsioids. When—"

"*Unh!*" Another graduate student jerked upright. While Methuen paused with his mouth open, a third man picked a small object off the floor and held it up.

"Really, gentlemen," said Methuen, "I thought you'd

outgrown such amusements as shooting rubber bands at
each other. As I was saying when—"

Wimpus gave another grunt and jerk. He glared about
him. Methuen tried to get his lecture going again. But, as
rubber bands from nowhere continued to sting the necks
and ears of the listeners, the classroom organization visibly
disintegrated like a lump of sugar in a cup of weak tea.

Johnny put on his spectacles and was peering about the
room. But he was no more successful than the others in lo-
cating the source of the bombardment.

He slid off his chair and shuffled over to the light
switch. The daylight through the windows left the rear end
of the classroom dark. As soon as the lights went on, the
source of the elastics was obvious. A couple of the graduates
pounced on a small wooden box on the shelf beside the projector.

The box gave out a faint whir, and spat rubber bands
through a slit, one every few seconds. They brought it up
and opened it on Methuen's lecture table. Inside was a mass
of machinery apparently made of the parts of a couple of
alarm clocks and a lot of hand-whittled wooden cams and
things.

"My, my," said Methuen. "A most ingenious contraption, isn't it?"

The machine ran down with a click. While they were
still examining it, the bell rang.

Methuen looked out the window. A September rain
was coming up. Ira Methuen pulled on his topcoat and his
rubbers and took his umbrella from the corner. He never
wore a hat. He went out and headed down Prospect Street,
Johnny padding behind.

"Hi!" said a young man, a fat young man in need of a
haircut. "Got any news for us, Professor Methuen?"

"I'm afraid not, Bruce," replied Methuen. "Unless you
call Ford's giant mouse news."

"What? What giant mouse?"

"Dr. Ford has produced a three-hundred-pound mouse

orthogonal mutation. He had to alter its morphological
aracteristics—"

"Its *what?*"

"Its shape, to you. He had to alter it to make it possible
r it to live—"

"Where? Where is it?"

"Osborn Labs. If—" But Bruce Inglehart was gone up
ie hill toward the science buildings. Methuen continued:
With no war on, and New Haven as dead a town as it al-
ays has been, they have to come to us for news, I suppose.
.ome on, Johnny. Getting garrulous in my old age."

A passing dog went crazy at the sight of Johnny, snarl-
ig and yelping. Johnny ignored it. They entered Wood-
ridge Hall.

Dr. Wendell Cook, president of Yale University, had
1ethuen sent in at once. Johnny, excluded from the sanc-
im, went up to the president's secretary. He stood up and
ut his paws on her desk. He leered—you have to see a bear
.er to know how it is done—and said, "How about it, kid?"

Miss Prescott, an unmistakable Boston spinster, smiled
t him. "Suttinly, Johnny. Just a moment." She finished typ-
ig a letter, opened a drawer, and took out a copy of Hecht's
Fantazius Mallare." This she gave Johnny. He curled up
n the floor, adjusted his glasses, and read.

After a while he looked up, saying: "Miss Prescott, I am
alfway srough zis, and I stirr don't see why zey cawr it ob-
cene. I sink it is just durr. Can't you get me a rearry dirty
ook?"

"Well, really, Johnny. I don't run a pornography shop,
ou know. Most people find that quite strong enough."

Johnny sighed. "Peopre get excited over ze funnies'
ings."

/leanwhile, Methuen was closeted with Cook and Dalrym-
le, the prospective endower, in another of those intermina-
le and indecisive conferences. R. Hanscom Dalrymple

looked like a statue that the sculptor had never got aroun
to finishing. The only expression the steel chairman ever a
lowed himself was a canny, secretive smile. Cook and M
thuen had a feeling he was playing them on the end of
long and well-knit fish line made of U.S. Federal Reserv
notes. It was not because he wasn't willing to part with th
damned endowment, but because he enjoyed the sensatio
of power over these oh-so-educated men. And in the actua
world, one doesn't lose one's temper and tell Croesus wha
to do with his loot. One says: "Yes, Mr. Dalrymple. My
my, that *is* a brilliant suggestion, Mr. Dalrymple! Wh
didn't we think of it ourselves?" Cook and Methuen wer
both old hands at this game. Methuen, though otherwise h
considered Wendell Cook a pompous ass, admired the pres
dent's endowment-snagging ability. After all, wasn't Yal
University named after a retired merchant on the basis of
gift of five hundred and sixty-two pounds twelve shillings?

"Say, Dr. Cook," said Dalrymple, "why don't you com
over to the Taft and have lunch on me for a change? You
too, Professor Methuen."

The academics murmured their delight and pulled o
their rubbers. On the way out Dalrymple paused to scratc
Johnny behind the ears. Johnny put his book away, keeping
the title on the cover out of sight, and restrained himsel
from snapping at the steel man's hand. Dalrymple mean
well enough, but Johnny did not like people to take such lib
erties with his person.

So the three men and a bear slopped down College
Street. Cook paused now and then, ignoring the sprinkle, to
make studied gestures toward one or another of the units o
the great soufflé of Georgian and Collegiate Gothic architec
ture. He explained this and that. Dalrymple merely smilec
his blank little smile.

Johnny, plodding behind, was the first to notice that
passing undergraduates were pausing to stare at the presi
dent's feet. The word "feet" is meant literally. For Cook's
rubbers were rapidly changing into a pair of enormous pink
bare feet.

Cook himself was quite unconscious of it, until quite a
roup of undergraduates had collected. These gave forth the
atarrhal snorts of men trying unsuccessfully not to laugh.
y the time Cook had followed their stares and looked
own, the metamorphosis was complete. That he should be
artled was only natural. The feet were startling enough.
lis face gradually matched the feet in redness, making a
reerful note of color in the gray landscape.

R. Hanscom Dalrymple lost his reserve for once. His
owls did nothing to save prexy's now-apoplectic face. Cook
nally stooped and pulled off the rubbers. It transpired that
re feet had been painted on the outside of the rubbers and
overed over with lampblack. The rain had washed the
ımpblack off.

Wendell Cook resumed his walk to the Hotel Taft in
loomy silence. He held the offensive rubbers between
rumb and finger as if they were something unclean and
oathsome. He wondered who had done this dastardly deed.
There hadn't been any undergraduates in his office for some
ays, but you never wanted to underestimate the ingenuity
f undergraduates. He noticed that Ira Methuen was wear-
ng rubbers of the same size and make as his own. But he
out suspicion in that direction out of his mind before it had
ully formed. Certainly Methuen wouldn't play practical
okes with Dalrymple around, when he'd be the head of the
New Department of Biophysics when—if—Dalrymple
ame through with the endowment.

The next man to suspect that the Yale campus was un-
lergoing a severe pixilation was John Dugan, the tall thin
ine of the two campus cops. He was passing Christ
Church—which is so veddy high-church Episcopal that they
efer to Charles I of England as St. Charles the Martyr—on
ris way to his lair in Phelps Tower. A still small voice spoke
n his ear: "Beware, John Dugan! Your sins will find you
out!"

Dugan jumped and looked around. The voice repeated
ts message. There was nobody within fifty feet of Dugan.
Moreover, he could not think of any really serious sins he

had committed lately. The only people in sight were a fer
undergraduates and Professor Methuen's educated blac
bear, trailing after his boss as usual. There was nothing fc
John Dugan to suspect but his own sanity.


R. Hanscom Dalrymple was a bit surprised at the grim eai
nestness of the professors in putting away their respectiv
shares of the James Pierpont dinner. They were staying th
eternal gnaw of hunger that afflicts those who depend on
college commissary for sustenance. Many of them suspecte
a conspiracy among the college cooks to see that the razo
edge wasn't taken off the students' and instructors' intel
lects by overfeeding. They knew that conditions were mucl
the same in most colleges.

Dalrymple sipped his coffee and looked at his notes
Presently Cook would get up and say a few pleasant noth
ings. Then he would announce Dalrymple's endowment
which was to be spent in building a Dalrymple Biophysica
Laboratory and setting up a new department. Everybod;
would applaud and agree that biophysics had floated in th
void between the domains of the departments of zoology
psychology, and the physiological sciences long enough
Then Dalrymple would get up and clear his throat anc
say—though in much more dignified language: "Shucks, fel
las, it really isn't nothing."

Dr. Wendell Cook duly got up, beamed out over the
ranked shirt fronts and said his pleasant nothings. The pro
fessors exchanged nervous looks when he showed signs o
going off into his favorite oration, there-is-no-conflict-be
tween-science-and-religion. They had heard it before.

He was well launched into Version 3A of this homily
when he began to turn blue in the face. It was not the dark
purplish-gray called loosely "blue" that appears on the face;
of stranglees, but a bright, cheerful cobalt. Now, such a col
or is all very well in a painting of a ship sailing under a clear
blue sky, or in the uniform of a movie-theater doorman. But
it is distinctly out of place in the face of a college president.

r so felt the professors. They leaned this way and that,
ieir boiled shirts bulging, popping and gaping as they did
), and whispered.

Cook frowned and continued. He was observed to sniff
ie air as if he smelled something. Those at the speakers' tale detected a slight smell of acetone. But that seemed hard-
' an adequate explanation of the robin's egg hue of their
rexy's face. The color was now quite solid on the face
roper. It ran up into the area where Cook's hair would
ave been if he had had some. His collar showed a trace of
, too.

Cook, on his part, had no idea of why the members of
is audience were swaying in their seats like saplings in a
ale and whispering. He thought it very rude of them. But
is frowns had no effect. So presently he cut Version 3A
iort. He announced the endowment in concise, business-
ke terms, and paused for the expected thunder of applause.

There was none. To be exact, there was a feeble patter
iat nobody in his right mind would call a thunder of any-
iing.

Cook looked at R. Hanscom Dalrymple, hoping that the
teel man would not be insulted. Dalrymple's face showed
othing. Cook assumed that this was part of his general re-
erve. The truth was that Dalrymple was too curious about
he blue face to notice the lack of applause. When Cook in-
roduced him to the audience, it took some seconds to pull
iimself together.

He started rather lamely. "Gentlemen and members of
he Yale faculty . . . uh . . . I mean, of course, you're *all* gen-
lemen . . . I am reminded of a story about the poultry farm-
r who got married—I mean, I'm not reminded of *that* story,
iut the one about the divinity student who died and went
o—" Here Dalrymple caught the eye of the dean of the di-
'inity school. He tacked again. "Maybe I'd . . . uh . . . better
ell the one about the Scotchman who got lost on his way
iome and—"

It was not a bad story, as such things go. But it got prac-
ically no laughter. Instead the professors began swaying,

like a roomful of boiled-shirted Eastern ascetics at thei
prayers, and whispering again.

Dalrymple could put two and two together. He leane
over and hissed into Cook's ear. "Is there anything wron
with me?"

"Yes, your face has turned green."

"Green?"

"Bright green. Like grass. Nice young grass."

"Well, you might like to know that yours is blue."

Both men felt their faces. There was no doubt; the
were masked with coatings of some sort of paint, still wet.

Dalrymple whispered: "What kind of gag is this?"

"I don't know. Better finish your speech."

Dalrymple tried. But his thoughts were scattered be
yond recovery. He made a few remarks about how glad h
was to be there amid the elms and ivy and traditions of ol
Eli, and sat down. His face looked rougher-hewn than ever
If a joke had been played on him—well, he hadn't signed
any checks yet.

The lieutenant governor of the State of Connecticu
was next on the list. Cook shot a question at him. He mum
bled: "But if I'm going to turn a funny color when I ge
up—"

The question of whether his honor should speak wa:
never satisfactorily settled. For at that moment a thing ap
peared on one end of the speakers' table. It was a beast the
size of a St. Bernard. It looked rather the way a common ba
would look if, instead of wings, it had arms with disk-shaped
pads on the ends of the fingers. Its eyes were as big aroun(
as luncheon plates.

There was commotion. The speaker sitting nearest the
thing fell over backward. The lieutenant governor crosse(
himself. An English zoologist put on his glasses and said
"By Jove, a spectral tarier! But a bit large, what?"

A natural-sized tarier would fit in your hand comfort
ably, and is rather cute if a bit spooky. But a tarier the size
of this one is not the kind of thing one can glance at and
then go on reading the adventures of Alley Oop. It break:

ne's train of thought. It disconcerts one. It may give one
ne screaming meemies.
   This tarier walked gravely down the twenty feet of tale. The diners were too busy going away from there to ob-
:rve that it upset no tumblers and kicked no ashtrays about;
nat it was, in fact, slightly transparent. At the other end of
ne table it vanished.


ohnny Black's curiosity wrestled with his better judgment.
lis curiosity told him that all these odd happenings had tak-
n place in the presence of Ira Methuen. Therefore, Ira Me-
nuen was at least a promising suspect. "So what?" his bet-
:r judgment said. "He's the only man you have a real
ffection for. If you learned that he was the pixie in the case,
ou wouldn't expose him, would you? Better keep your
nuzzle out of this."
   But in the end his curiosity won, as usual. The wonder
/as that his better judgment kept on trying.
   He got hold of Bruce Inglehart. The young reporter
ad a reputation for discretion.
   Johnny explained: "He gave himserf ze Messuen treat-
nent—you know, ze spinar injection—to see what it would
o to a man. Zat was a week ago. Should have worked by
ow. He says it had no effec'. Maybe not. But day after ze
ose, awr zese sings start happening. Ver eraborate jokes.
<ind a crazy scientific genius would do. If it's him, I mus'
top him before he makes rear troubre. You wirr he'p me?"
   "Sure, Johnny. Shake on it."
   Johnny extended a paw.


t was two nights later that Durfee Hall caught fire. Yale
ad been discussing the erasure of this singularly ugly and
seless building for forty years. It had been vacant for some
ime, except for the bursar's office in the basement.
   About ten o'clock an undergraduate noticed little red
ongues of flame crawling up the roof. He gave the alarm at

once. The New Haven fire department was not to I
blamed for the fact that the fire spread as fast as if the buil
ing had been soaked in kerosene. By the time they, an
about a thousand spectators, had arrived, the whole cent
of the building was going up with a fine roar and crackl
The assistant bursar bravely dashed into the building an
reappeared with an armful of papers, which later turned ou
to be a pile of quite useless examination forms. The fire de
partment squirted enough water onto the burning section t
put out Mount Vesuvius. Some of them climbed ladders a
the ends of the building to chop holes in the roof.

The water seemed to have no effect. So the fire depar
ment called for some more apparatus, connected up mor
hoses, and squirted more water. The undergraduates yellec

"Rah, rah, fire department! Rah, rah, fire! Go get 'en
department! Hold that line, fire!"

Johnny Black bumped into Bruce Inglehart, who wa
dodging about in the crowd with a pad and pencil, trying t
get information for his New Haven *Courier*. Inglehart aske
Johnny whether he knew anything.

Johnny, in his deliberate manner, said: "I know on
sing. Zat is ze firs' hetress fire I have seen."

Inglehart looked at Johnny, then at the conflagration
"My gosh!" he said. "We ought to feel the radiation here
oughtn't we? Heatless fire is right. Another superscientifi
joke, you suppose?"

"We can rook around," said Johnny. Turning thei
backs on the conflagration, they began searching among th
shrubbery and railings along Elm Street.

"Woof!" said Johnny. "Come here, Bruce!"

In a patch of shadow stood Professor Ira Methuen and i
tripod whereon was mounted a motion-picture projector. I
took Johnny a second to distinguish which was which.

Methuen seemed uneasily poised on the verge of flight
He said: "Why, hello, Johnny; why aren't you asleep? I jus
found this . . . uh . . . this projector—"

Johnny, thinking fast, slapped the projector with hi
paw. Methuen caught it as it toppled. Its whir ceased. At th
same instant the fire went out, vanished utterly. The roa

and crackle still came from the place where the fire had been. But there was no fire. There was not even a burned place in the roof, off which gallons of water were still pouring. The fire department looked at one another foolishly.

While Johnny's and Inglehart's pupils were still expanding in the sudden darkness, Methuen and his projector vanished. They got a glimpse of him galloping around the College Street corner, lugging the tripod. They ran after him. A few undergraduates ran after Johnny and Inglehart, being moved by the instinct that makes dogs chase automobiles.

They caught sight of Methuen, lost him, and caught sight of him again. Inglehart was not built for running, and Johnny's eyesight was an affair of limited objectives. Johnny opened up when it became evident that Methuen was heading for the old Phelps mansion, where he, Johnny, and several unmarried instructors lived. Everybody in the house had gone to see the fire. Methuen dashed in the front door three jumps ahead of Johnny and slammed it in the bear's face.

Johnny padded around in the dark with the idea of attacking a window. But while he was making up his mind, something happened to the front steps under him. They became slicker than the smoothest ice. Down the steps went Johnny, *bump-bump-bump.*

Johnny picked himself up in no pleasant mood. So this was the sort of treatment he got from the one man— But then, he reflected, if Methuen was really crazy, you couldn't blame him.


Some of the undergraduates caught up with them. These crowded toward the mansion—until their feet went out from under them as if they were wearing invisible roller skates. They tried to get up, and fell again, sliding down the slight grade of the crown of the road into heaps in the gutter. They retired on hands and knees, their clothes showing large holes.

A police car drove up and tried to stop. Apparently nei-

ther brakes nor tires would hold. It skidded about, banged
against the curb once, and finally stopped down the street
beyond the slippery-zone. The cop—he was a fairly important cop, a captain—got out and charged the mansion.

He fell down, too. He tried to keep going on hands and
knees. But every time he applied a horizontal component of
force to a hand or knee, the hand or knee simply slid backward. The sight reminded Johnny of the efforts of those gar-
ter snakes to crawl on the smooth concrete floor of the Central Park Zoo monkey house.

When the police captain gave up and tried to retreat,
the laws of friction came back on. But when he stood up, all
his clothes below the waist, except his shoes, disintegrated
into a cloud of textile fibers.

"My word!" said the English zoologist, who had just arrived. "Just like one of those Etruscan statues, don't you
know!"

The police captain bawled at Bruce Inglehart: "Hey,
you, for gossakes gimmie a handkerchief!"

"What's the matter; got a cold?" asked Inglehart inno-
cently.

"No, you dope! You know what I want it for!"

Inglehart suggested that a better idea would be for the
captain to use his coat as an apron. While the captain was
knotting the sleeves behind his back, Inglehart and Johnny
explained their version of the situation to him.

"Hm-m-m," said the captain. "We don't want nobody
to get hurt, or the place to get damaged. But suppose he's
got a death ray or sumpm?"

"I don't sink so," said Johnny. "He has not hurt anybody. Jus' prayed jokes."

The captain thought for a few seconds of ringing up
headquarters and having them send an emergency truck.
But the credit for overpowering a dangerous maniac single-
handed was too tempting. He said: "How'll we get into the
place, if he can make everything so slippery?"

They thought. Johnny said: "Can you get one of zose

sings wiss a wood stick and a rubber cup on end?"

The captain frowned. Johnny made motions. Inglehart said: "Oh, you mean the plumber's friend! Sure. You wait. I'll get one. See if you can find a key to the place."

The assault on Methuen's stronghold was made on all fours. The captain, in front, jammed the end of the plumber's friend against the rise of the lowest front step. If Methuen could abolish friction, he had not discovered how to get rid of barometric pressure. The rubber cup held, and the cop pulled himself, Inglehart and Johnny after him. By using the instrument on successive steps, they mounted them. Then the captain anchored them to the front door and pulled them up to it. He hauled himself to his feet by the door handle, and opened the door with a key borrowed from Dr. Wendell Cook.

At one window Methuen crouched behind a thing like a surveyor's transit. He swiveled the thing toward them, and made adjustments. The captain and Inglehart, feeling their shoes grip the floor, gathered themselves to jump. But Methuen got the contraption going, and their feet went from under them.

Johnny used his head. He was standing next to the door. He lay down, braced his hind feet against the door frame, and kicked out. His body whizzed across the frictionless floor and bowled over Methuen and his contraption.

The professor offered no more resistance. He seemed more amused than anything, despite the lump that was growing on his forehead. He said: "My, my, you fellows *are* persistent. I suppose you're going to take me off to some asylum. I thought you and you"— he indicated Inglehart and Johnny— "were my friends. Oh, well, it doesn't matter."

The captain growled: "What did you do to my pants?"

"Simple. My telubricator here neutralizes the interatomic bonds on the surface of any solid on which the beam falls. So the surface, to a depth of a few molecules, is put in the condition of a supercooled liquid as long as the beam is focused on it. Since the liquid form of any compound will wet the solid form, you have perfect lubrication."

"But my pants—"

"They were held together by friction between the fibers, weren't they? And I have a lot more inventions like that. My soft-speaker and my three-dimensional projector, for instance, are—"

Inglehart interrupted: "Is that how you made that phony fire, and that whatchamicallit that scared the people at the dinner? With a three-dimensional projector?"

"Yes, of course, though, to be exact, it took two projectors at right angles, and a phonograph and amplifier to give the sound effect. It was amusing, wasn't it?"

"But," wailed Johnny, "why do you do zese sings? You trying to ruin your career?"

Methuen shrugged. "It doesn't matter. Nothing matters, Johnny, as you'd know if you were in my ... uh ... condition. And now, gentlemen, where do you want me to go? Wherever it is, I'll find something amusing there."


Dr. Wendell Cook visited Ira Methuen on the first day of his incarceration in the New Haven Hospital. In ordinary conversation Methuen seemed sane enough, and quite agreeable. He readily admitted that he had been the one responsible for the jokes. He explained: "I painted your and Dalrymple's faces with a high-powered needle sprayer I invented. It's a most amusing little thing. Fits in your hand and discharges through a ring on your finger. With your thumb you can regulate the amount of acetone mixed in with the water, which in turn controls the surface tension and therefore the point at which the needle spray breaks up into droplets. I made the spray break up just before it reached your face. You were a sight, Cook, especially when you found out what was wrong with you. You looked almost as funny as the day I painted those feet on my rubbers and substituted them for yours. You react so beautifully to having your dignity pricked. You always were a pompous ass, you know."

Cook puffed out his cheeks and controlled himself. After all, the poor man was mad. These absurd outbursts about Cook's pompousness proved it. He said sadly: "Dalrymple's leaving tomorrow night. He was most displeased about the face-painting episode, and when he found that you were under observation, he told me that no useful purpose would be served by his remaining here. I'm afraid that's the end of our endowment. Unless you can pull yourself together and tell us what's happened to you and how to cure it."

Ira Methuen laughed. "Pull myself together? I am all in one piece, I assure you. And I've told you what's the matter with me, as you put it. I gave myself my own treatment. As for curing it, I wouldn't tell you how even if I knew. I wouldn't give up my present condition for anything. I at last realize that nothing really matters, including endowments. I shall be taken care of, and I will devote myself to amusing myself as I see fit."

Johnny had been haunting Cook's office all day. He waylaid the president when the latter returned from the hospital.

Cook told Johnny what had happened. He said: "He seems to be completely irresponsible. We'll have to get in touch with his son, and have a guardian appointed. And we'll have to do something about you, Johnny."

Johnny didn't relish the prospect of the "something." He knew he had no legal status other than that of a tamed wild animal. The fact that Methuen technically owned him was his only protection if somebody took a notion to shoot him during bear-hunting season. And he was not enthusiastic about Ralph Methuen. Ralph was a very average young schoolteacher without his father's scientific acumen or whimsical humor. Finding Johnny on his hands, his reaction would be to give Johnny to a zoo or something.

He put his paws on Miss Prescott's desk and asked: "Hey, good-rooking, wirr you cawr up Bruce Ingrhart at ze *Courier?*"

"Johnny," said the president's secretary, "you get fresher every day."

"Ze bad infruence of ze undergraduates. Wirr you cawr Mr. Ingrehart, beautifur?" Miss Prescott, who was not, did so.

Bruce Inglehart arrived at the Phelps mansion to find Johnny taking a shower. Johnny was also making a horrible bawling noise. "*Waaaa!*" he howled. "*Hooooooo! Yrrrrrr! Waaaaaa!*"

"Watcha doing?" yelled Inglehart.

"Taking a bass," replied Johnny. "*Wuuuuuuh!*"

"Are you sick?"

"No, jus' singing in bass. Peopre sing whire taking bass; why shouldn't I? *Yaaaaaaa!*"

"Well, for Pete's sake don't. It sounds like you were having your throat cut. What's the idea of these bath towels spread all over the floor?"

"I show you." Johnny came out of the shower, lay down on the bath towels and rolled. When he was more or less dry, he scooped the towels up in his forepaws and heaved them in a corner. Neatness was not one of Johnny's strong points.

He told Inglehart about the Methuen situation. "Rook here, Bruce," he said. "I sink I can fix him, but you wirr have to he'p me."

"O.K. Count me in."


*Pop!*

The orderly looked up from his paper. But none of the buttons showed a light. So, presumably, none of the patients wanted attention. He went back to his reading.

*Pop!*

It sounded a little like a breaking light bulb. The orderly sighed, put away his paper, and began prowling. As he approached the room of the mad professor, No. 14, he noticed a smell of limburger.

*Pop!*

There was no doubt that the noise came from No. 14. The orderly stuck his head in.

At one side of the room sat Ira Methuen. He held a contraption made of a length of glass rod and assorted wire. At the other side of the room on the floor, lay a number of crumbs of cheese. A cockroach scuttled out of the shadows and made for the crumbs. Methuen sighted along his glass rod and pressed a button. *Pop!* A flash, and there was no more cockroach.

Methuen swung the rod toward the orderly. "Stand back, sir! I'm Buck Rogers, and this is my disintegrator!"

"Hey," said the orderly feebly. The old goof might be crazy, but after what happened to the roach— He ducked out and summoned a squad of interns.

But the interns had no trouble with Methuen. He tossed the contraption on the bed, saying: "If I thought it mattered, I'd raise a hell of a stink about cockroaches in a supposedly sanitary hospital."

One of the interns protested: "But I'm sure there aren't any here."

"What do you call that?" asked Methuen dryly, pointing at the shattered remains of one of his victims.

"It must have been attracted in from the outside by the smell of that cheese. *Phew!* Judson, clean up the floor. What *is* this, professor?" He picked up the rod and the flashlight battery attached to it.

Methuen waved a deprecating hand. "Nothing important. Just a little gadget I thought up. By applying the right e.m.f. to pure crown glass, it's possible to raise its index of refraction to a remarkable degree. The result is that light striking the glass is so slowed up that it takes weeks to pass through it in the ordinary manner. The light that is thus trapped can be released by making a small spark near the glass. So I simply lay the rod on the window sill all afternoon to soak up sunlight, a part of which is released by making a spark with the button. Thus I can shoot an hour's accumulated light-energy out from the front end of the rod in a very small fraction of a second. Naturally, when this beam hits an opaque object, it raises its temperature. So I've been amusing myself by luring the roaches in here and exploding them. You may have the thing; its charge is about exhausted."

The intern was stern. "That's a dangerous weapon. We can't let you play with things like that."

"Oh, can't you? Not that it matters, but I'm only staying here because I'm taken care of. I can walk out any time I like."

"No you can't, professor. You're under a temporary commitment for observation."

"That's all right, son. I still say I can walk out whenever I feel like it. I just don't care much whether I do or not." With which Methuen began tuning the radio by his bed, ignoring the interns.


Exactly twelve hours later, at 10 A.M., Ira Methuen's room in the hospital was found to be vacant. A search of the hospital failed to locate him. The only clue to his disappearance was the fact that his radio had been disemboweled. Tubes, wires, and condensers lay in untidy heaps on the floor.

The New Haven police cars received instructions to look for a tall, thin man with gray hair and goatee, probably armed with death rays, disintegrators, and all the other advanced weapons of fact and fiction.

For hours they scoured the city with screaming sirens. They finally located the menacing madman, sitting placidly on a park bench three blocks from the hospital and reading a newspaper. Far from resisting, he grinned at them and looked at his watch. "Three hours and forty-eight minutes. Not bad, boys, not bad, considering how carefully I hid myself."

One of the cops pounced on a bulge in Methuen's pocket. The bulge was made by another wire contraption. Methuen shrugged. "My hyperbolic solenoid. Gives you a conical magnetic field, and enables you to manipulate ferrous objects at a distance. I pick the lock of the door to the elevators with it."

When Bruce Inglehart arrived at the hospital about four, he was told Methuen was asleep. That was amended to the statement that Methuen was getting up, and could see a visitor in a few minutes. He found Methuen in a dressing gown.

Methuen said: "Hello, Bruce. They had me wrapped up in a wet sheet, like a mummy. It's swell for naps; relaxes you. I told 'em they could do it whenever they liked. I think they were annoyed about my getting out."

Inglehart was slightly embarrassed.

Methuen said: "Don't worry; I'm not mad at you. I realize that nothing matters, including resentments. And I've had a most amusing time here. Just watch them fizz the next time I escape."

"But don't you care about your future?" said Inglehart. "They'll transfer you to a padded cell at Middletown—"

Methuen waved a hand. "That doesn't bother me. I'll have fun there, too."

"But how about Johnny Black, and Dalrymple's endowment?"

"I don't give a damn what happens to them."

Here the orderly stuck his head in the door briefly to check up on this unpredictable patient. The hospital, being short-handed, was unable to keep a continuous watch on him.

Methuen continued: "Not that I don't like Johnny. But when you get a real sense of proportion, like mine, you realize that humanity is nothing but a sort of skin disease on a ball of dirt, and that no effort beyond subsistence, shelter, and casual amusement is worthwhile. The State of Connecticut is willing to provide the first two for me, so I shall devote myself to the third. What's that you have there?"

Inglehart thought, "They're right; he's become a childishly irresponsible scientific genius." Keeping his back to the door, the reporter brought out his family heirloom: a big silver pocket flask dating back to the fabulous prohibition period. His Aunt Martha had left it to him, and he himself expected to will it to a museum.

"Apricot brandy," he murmured. Johnny had tipped him off to Methuen's tastes.

"Now, Bruce, that's something sensible. Why didn't you bring it out sooner, instead of making futile appeals to my sense of duty?"


The flask was empty. Ira Methuen sprawled in his chair. Now and then he passed a hand across his forehead. He said: "I can't believe it. I can't believe that I felt that way half an hour ago. O Lord, what have I done?"

"Plenty," said Inglehart.

Methuen was not acting at all drunk. He was full of sober remorse.

"I remember everything—those inventions that popped out of my mind, everything. But I didn't care. How did you know alcohol would counteract the Methuen injection?"

"Johnny figured it out. He looked up its effects, and discovered that in massive doses it coagulates the proteins in the nerve cells. He guessed it would lower their conductivity to counteract the increased conductivity through the gaps between them that your treatment causes."

"So," said Methuen, "when I'm sober I'm drunk, and when I'm drunk I'm sober. But what'll we do about the endowment—my new department and the laboratory and everything?"

"I don't know. Dalrymple's leaving tonight; he had to stay over a day on account of some trustee business. And they won't let you out for a while yet, even when they know about the alcohol counter-treatment. Better think of something quick, because the visiting period is pretty near up."

Methuen thought. He said: "I remember how all those inventions work, though I couldn't possibly invent any more of them unless I went back to the other condition." He shuddered. "There's the soft-speaker, for instance—"

"What's that?"

"It's like a loud-speaker, only it doesn't speak loudly. It throws a supersonic beam, modulated by the human voice to give the effect of audible sound-frequencies when it hits the human ear. Since you can throw a supersonic beam almost as accurately as you can throw a light beam, you can turn the soft-speaker on a person, who will then hear a still small voice in his ear apparently coming from nowhere. I tried it on Dugan one day. It worked. Could you do anything with that?"

"I don't know. Maybe."

"I hope you can. This is terrible. I thought I was perfectly sane and rational. Maybe I was— Maybe nothing is important. But I don't feel that way now, and I don't want to feel that way again—"

The omnipresent ivy, of which Yale is so proud, affords splendid handholds for climbing. Bruce Inglehart, keeping an eye peeled for campus cops, swarmed up the big tower at the corner of Bingham Hall. Below, in the dark, Johnny waited.

Presently the end of a clothesline came dangling down. Johnny inserted the hook in the end of the rope ladder into the loop in the end of the line. Inglehart hauled the ladder up and secured it, wishing that he and Johnny could change bodies for a while. That climb up the ivy had scared him and winded him badly. But he could climb ivy and Johnny couldn't.

The ladder creaked under Johnny's five hundred pounds. A few minutes later it slid slowly, jerkily up the wall, like a giant centipede. Then Inglehart, Johnny, ladder, and all were on top of the tower.

Inglehart got out the soft-speaker and trained the telescopic sight on the window of Dalrymple's room in the Taft, across the intersection of College and Chapel Streets. He found the yellow rectangle of light. He could see in about half the room. His heart skipped a few beats until a stocky figure moved into his field of vision. Dalrymple had not yet left. But he was packing a couple of suitcases.

Inglehart slipped the transmitter clip around his neck, so that the transmitter nestled against his larynx. The next time Dalrymple appeared, Inglehart focused the cross-hairs on the steel man's head. He spoke: "Hanscom Dalrymple!" He saw the man stop suddenly. He repeated: "Hanscom Dalrymple!"

"Huh?" said Dalrymple. "Who the hell are you? Where the hell are you?" Inglehart could not hear him, of course, but he could guess.

Inglehart said, in solemn tones: "I am your conscience."

By now Dalrymple's agitation was evident even at that distance. Inglehart continued: "Who squeezed out all the common stockholders of Hephaestus Steel in that phony re-organization?" Pause. "You did, Hanscom Dalrymple!

"Who bribed a United States senator to swing the vote for a higher steel tariff, with fifty thousand dollars and a promise of fifty thousand more, which was never paid?" Pause. "You did, Hanscom Dalrymple!

"Who promised Wendell Cook the money for a new biophysics building, and then let his greed get the better of him and backed out on the thin excuse that the man who was to have headed the new department had had a nervous breakdown?" Pause, while Inglehart reflected that "nervous breakdown" was merely a nice way of saying "gone nuts." "You did, Hanscom Dalrymple!

"Do you know what'll happen to you if you don't atone, Dalrymple? You'll be reincarnated as a spider, and probably caught by a wasp and used as live fodder for her larvae. How will you like that, *heh-heh?*

"What can you do to atone? Don't be a sap. Call up Cook. Tell him you've changed your mind and are renewing your offer!" Pause. "Well, what are you waiting for? Tell him you're not only renewing it, but doubling it!" Pause. "Tell him—"

But at this point Dalrymple moved swiftly to the telephone. Inglehart said, "Ah, that's better, Dalrymple," and shut off the machine.

Johnny asked: "How did you know awr zose sings about him?"

"I got belief in reincarnation out of his obit down at the shop. And one of our rewrite men who used to work in Washington says everybody down there knows about the other things. Only you can't print a thing like that unless you have evidence to back it up."

They lowered the rope ladder and reversed the process by which they had come up. They gathered up their stuff and started for the Phelps mansion. But as they rounded the corner of Bingham they almost ran into a familiar stork-like figure. Methuen was just setting up another contraption at the corner of Welch.

"Hello," he said.

Man and bear gaped at him. Inglehart asked: "Did you escape again?"

"Uh-huh. When I sobered up and got my point of view back. It was easy, even though they'd taken my radio away. I invented a hypnotizer, using a light bulb and a rheostat made of wire from my mattress, and hypnotized the orderly into giving me his uniform and opening the doors for me. My, my, that *was* amusing."

"What are you doing now?" Inglehart became aware that Johnny's black pelt had melted off in the darkness.

"This? Oh, I dropped around home and knocked together an improved soft-speaker. This one'll work through masonry walls. I'm going to put all the undergraduates to sleep and tell 'em they're monkeys. When they wake up, it will be most amusing to see them running around on all fours and scratching and climbing the chandeliers. They're practically monkeys to begin with, so it shouldn't be difficult."

"But you can't, professor! Johnny and I just went to a lot of trouble getting Dalrymple to renew his offer. You don't want to let us down, do you?"

"What you and Johnny do doesn't matter to me in the slightest. Nothing matters. I'm going to have my fun. And don't try to interfere, Bruce." Methuen pointed another glass rod at Inglehart's middle. "You're a nice young fellow, and it would be too bad if I had to let you have three hours' accumulation of sun-ray energy all at once."

"But this afternoon you said—"

"I know what I said this afternoon. I was drunk and back in my old state of mind, full of responsibility and conscientiousness and such bunk. I'll never touch the stuff again if it has that effect on me. Only a man who has received the Methuen treatment can appreciate the futility of all human effort."

Methuen shrank back into the shadows as a couple of undergraduates passed. Then he resumed work on his contraption, using one hand and keeping Inglehart covered with the other. Inglehart, not knowing what else to do, asked him questions about the machine. Methuen responded with a string of technical jargon. Inglehart wondered desperately what to do. He was not an outstandingly brave young man, especially in the face of a gun or its equivalent. Methuen's bony hand never wavered. He made the adjustments on his machine mostly by feel.

"Now," he said, "that ought to be about right. This contains a tonic metronome that will send them a note on a frequency of 349 cycles a second, with 68.4 pulses of sound a minute. This, for various technical reasons, has the maximum hypnotic effect. From here I can rake the colleges along College Street—" He made a final adjustment. "This will be the most amusing joke yet. And the cream of it is that, since Connecticut is determined to consider me insane, they can't do anything to me for it! Here goes, Bruce—*Phew*, has somebody started a still here, or what? I've been smelling and tasting alcohol for the last five minutes—*ouch!*"

The glass rod gave one dazzling flash, and then Johnny's hairy black body catapulted out of the darkness. Down went Ira Methuen, all the wind knocked out of him.

"Quick, Bruce!" barked Johnny. "Pick up zar needre sprayer I dropped. Unscrew ze container on ze bottom. Don't spirr it. Zen come here and pour it down his sroat!"

This was done, with Johnny holding Methuen's jaws .part with his claws, like Sampson slaying the lion, only :onversely.

They waited a few minutes for the alcohol to take ef- 'ect, listening for sounds that they had been discovered. But he colleges were silent save for the occasional tick of a type- vriter.

Johnny explained: "I ran home and got ze needre spray- :r from his room. Zen I got Webb, ze research assistant in iophysics, to ret me in ze raboratory for ze arcohor. Zen I 'neak up and squirt a spray in his mouse whire he talks. I ;et some in, but I don't get ze sprayer adjusted right, and ze ;pray hit him before it breaks up, and stings him. I don't 1ave fingers, you know. So we have to use what ze books :awr brute force."

Methuen began to show signs of normalcy. As without 1is glass rod he was just a harmless old professor, Johnny let 1im up. His words tumbled out: "I'm so glad you did, John- 1y—you saved my reputation, maybe my life. Those fat- 1eads at the hospital wouldn't believe I had to be kept full of alcohol, so, of course, I sobered up and went crazy again— maybe they'll believe me now. Come on; let's get back there quickly. If they haven't discovered my absence, they might be willing to keep this last escape quiet. When they let me but, I'll work on a permanent cure for the Methuen treat- ment. I'll find it, if I don't die of stomach ulcers from all the alcohol I'll have to drink."

Johnny waddled up Temple Street to his home, feeling rath- er smug about his ability as a fixer. Maybe Methuen, sober, was right about the futility of it all. But if such a philosophy led to the upsetting of pleasant existence, Johnny preferred Methuen drunk.

He was glad Methuen would soon be well and coming home. Methuen was the only man he had any sentimental regard for. But as long as Methuen was shut up, Johnny was going to take advantage of that fact. When he reached the

Phelps mansion, instead of going directly in, he thrust a foreleg around behind the hedge next to the wall. It came out with a huge slab of chewing tobacco. Johnny bit off about half the slab, thrust the rest back in its cache, and went in, drooling happily a little at each step. Why not?

# Wolves Don't Cry

## by Bruce Elliott

The Naked Man behind the bars was sound asleep. In the cage next to him a bear rolled over on its back, and peered sleepily at the rising sun. Not far away a jackal paced springily back and forth as though essaying the impossible, trying to leave its own stench far behind.

Flies were gathered around the big bone that rested near the man's sleeping head. Little bits of decaying flesh attracted the insects and their hungry buzzing made the man stir uneasily. Accustomed to instant awakening, his eyes flickered and simultaneously his right hand darted out and smashed down at the irritating flies.

They left in a swarm, but the naked man stayed frozen in the position he had assumed. His eyes were on his hand.

He was still that way when the zoo attendant came close to the cage. The attendant, a pail of food in one hand, a pail of water in the other, said, "Hi Lobo, up and at 'em, the customers'll be here soon." Then he too froze.

Inside the naked man's head strange ideas were stirring. His paw, what had happened to it? Where was the stiff gray hair? The jet-black steel-strong nails? And what was the odd fifth thing that jutted out from his paw at right angles? He moved it experimentally. It rotated. He'd never been able to move his dewclaw, and the fact that he could move this fifth extension was somehow more baffling than the other oddities that were puzzling him.

"You goddamn drunks!" the attendant raved. "Wasn't bad enough the night a flock of you came in here, and a girl bothered the bear and lost an arm for her trouble, no that wasn't bad enough. Now you have to sleep in my cages! And where's Lobo? What have you done with him?"

The naked figure wished the two-legged would stop barking. It was enough trouble trying to figure out what had happened without the angry short barks of the two-legged who fed him interfering with his thoughts.

Then there were many more of the two-leggeds and a lot of barking, and the naked one wished they'd all go away and let him think. Finally the cage was opened and the two-leggeds tried to make him come out of his cage. He retreated hurriedly on all fours to the back of his cage towards his den.

"Let him alone," the two-legged who fed him barked. "Let him go into Lobo's den. He'll be sorry!"

Inside the den, inside the hollowed-out rock that so cleverly approximated his home before he had been captured, he paced back and forth, finding it bafflingly uncomfortable to walk on his naked feet. His paws did not grip the ground the way they should and the rock hurt his new soft pads.

The two-legged ones were getting angry, he could smell the emotion as it poured from them, but even that was puzzling, for he had to flare his nostrils wide to get the scent, and it was blurred, not crisp and clear the way he ordinarily smelled things. Throwing back his head, he howled in frustration and anger. But the sound was wrong. It did not ululate as was its wont. Instead he found to his horror that he sounded like a cub, or a female.

What had happened to him?

Cutting one of his soft pads on a stone, he lifted his foot and licked at the blood.

His pounding heart almost stopped.

This was no wolf blood.

Then the two-legged ones came in after him and the fight was one that ordinarily he would have enjoyed, but now his heart was not in it. Dismay filled him, for the taste of his own blood had put fear in him. Fear unlike any he had ever known, even when he was trapped that time, and put in a box, and thrown onto a wheeled thing that had rocked back and forth, and smelled so badly of two-legged things.

This was a new fear, and a horrible one.

Their barking got louder when they found that he was alone in his den. Over and over they barked, not that he could understand them, "What have you done with Lobo? Where is he? Have you turned him loose?"

It was only after a long time, when the sun was riding high in the summer sky, that he was wrapped in a foul-smelling thing and put in a four-wheeled object and taken away from his den.

He would never have thought, when he was captured, that he would ever miss the new home that the two-leggeds had given him, but he found that he did, and most of all, as the four-wheeled thing rolled through the city streets, he found himself worrying about his mate in the next cage. What would she think when she found him gone, and she just about to have a litter? He knew that most mates did not worry about their young, but wolves were different. No mother wolf ever had to worry, the way female bears did, about a male wolf eating his young. No indeed; wolves were different.

And being different, he found that worse than being tied up in a cloth and thrown in the back of a long, wheeled thing was the worry he felt about his mate, and her young-to-be.

But worse was to come: When he was carried out of the moving thing, the two-legged ones carried him into a big building and the smells that surged in on his outraged nostrils literally made him cringe. There was sickness, and stenches worse than he had ever smelled, and above and beyond all other smells the odor of death was heavy in the long white corridors through which he was carried.

Seeing around him as he did ordinarily in grays and blacks and whites, he found that the new sensations that crashed against his smarting eyeballs were not to be explained by anything he knew. Not having the words for red, and green, and yellow, for pink and orange and all the other colors in a polychromatic world, not having any idea of what they were, just served to confuse him even more miserably.

He moaned.

The smells, the discomfort, the horror of being handled, were as nothing against the hurt his eyes were enduring.

Lying on a flat hard thing he found that it helped just to stare directly upwards. At least the flat covering ten feet above him was white, and he could cope with that.

The two-legged thing sitting next to him had a gentle bark, but that didn't help much.

The two-legged said patiently over and over again, "Who are you? Have you any idea? Do you know where you are? What day is this?"

After a while the barks became soothing, and nude no longer, wrapped now in a long wet sheet that held him cocoonlike in its embrace, he found that his eyes were closing. It was all too much for him.

He slept.

The next awakening was if anything worse than the first.

First he thought that he was back in his cage in the zoo, for directly ahead of him he could see bars. Heaving a sigh of vast relief, he wondered what had made an adult wolf have such an absurd dream. He could still remember his puppyhood when sleep had been made peculiar by a life unlike the one he enjoyed when awake. The twitchings, the growls, the sleepy murmurs—he had seen his own sons and daughters go through them and they had reminded him of his youth.

But now the bars were in front of him and all was well.

Except that he must have slept in a peculiar position. He was stiff, and when he went to roll over he fell off the hard thing he had been on and crashed to the floor.

Bars or no bars, this was not his cage.

That was what made the second awakening so difficult. For, once he had fallen off the hospital bed, he found that his limbs were encumbered by a long garment that flapped around him as he rolled to all fours and began to pace fearfully back and forth inside the narrow confines of the cell that he now inhabited.

Worse yet, when the sound of his fall reached the ears of a two-legged one, he found that some more two-legs hurried to his side and he was forced, literally forced into an odd garment that covered his lower limbs.

Then they made him sit on the end of his spine and it hurt cruelly, and they put a metal thing in his right paw, and wrapped the soft flesh of his paw around the metal object and holding both, they made him lift some kind of slop from a round thing on the flat surface in front of him.

That was bad, but the taste of the mush they forced into his mouth was grotesque.

Where was his meat? Where was his bone? How could he sharpen his fangs on such food as this? What were they trying to do? Make him lose his teeth?

He gagged and regurgitated the slops. That didn't do the slightest bit of good. The two-leggeds kept right on forcing the mush into his aching jaws. Finally, in despair, he kept some of it down.

Then they made him balance on his hind legs.

He'd often seen the bear in the next cage doing this trick and sneered at the big fat oaf for pandering to the two-leggeds by aping them. Now he found that it was harder than he would have thought. But finally, after the two-leggeds had worked with him for a long time, he found that he could, by much teetering, stand erect.

But he didn't like it.

His nose was too far from the floor, and with whatever was wrong with his smelling, he found that he had trouble sniffing the ground under him. From this distance he could not track anything. Not even a rabbit. If one had run right by him, he thought, feeling terribly sorry for himself, he'd never be able to smell it, or if he did, be able to track it down, no matter how fat and juicy, for how could a wolf run on two legs?

They did many things to him in the new big zoo, and in time he found that, dislike it as much as he did, they could force him by painful expedients to do many of the tasks they set him.

That, of course, did not help him to understand why they wanted him to do such absurd things as encumber his legs with cloth that flapped and got in the way, or balance precariously on his hind legs, or any of the other absurdities they made him perform. But somehow he surmounted everything and in time even learned to bark a little the way they did. He found that he could bark *hello* and *I'm hungry* and, after months of effort, ask *why can't I go back to the zoo?*

But that didn't do much good, because all they ever barked back was *because you're a man.*

Now of many things he was unsure since that terrible morning, but of one thing he was sure: he *was* a wolf.

Other people knew it too.

He found this out on the day some outsiders were let into the place where he was being kept. He had been sitting, painful as it was, on the tip of his spine, in what he had found the two-leggeds called a chair, when some shes passed by.

His nostrils closed at the sweet smell that they had poured on themselves, but through it he could detect the real smell, the female smell, and his nostrils had flared, and he had run to the door of his cell, and his eyes had become red as he looked at them. Not so attractive as his mate, but at least they were covered with fur, not like the peeled ones that he sometimes saw dressed in stiff white crackling things.

The fur-covered ones had giggled just like ripening she-cubs, and his paws had ached to grasp them, and his jaws ached to bite into their fur-covered necks.

One of the fur-covered two-leggeds had giggled, "Look at that wolf!"

So some of the two-leggeds had perception and could tell that the ones who held him in this big strange zoo were wrong, that he was not a man, but a wolf.

Inflating his now puny lungs to the utmost he had thrown back his head and roared out a challenge that in the old days, in the forest, would have sent a thrill of pleasure through every female for miles around. But instead of the blood-curdling, stomach-wrenching roar, a little barking, choking sound came from his throat. If he had still had a tail it would have curled down under his belly as he slunk away.

The first time they let him see himself in what they called a mirror he had moaned like a cub. Where was his long snout, the bristling whiskers, the flat head, the pointed ears? What was this thing that stared with dilated eyes out of the flat shiny surface? White-faced, almost hairless save for a jet-black bar of eyebrows that made a straight line across his high round forehead, small-jawed, small-toothed—he knew with a sinking sensation in the pit of his stomach that even a year-old would not hesitate to challenge him in the mating fights.

Not only challenge him but beat him, for how could he fight with those little canines, those feeble white hairless paws?

Another thing that irritated him, as it would any wolf, was that they kept moving him around. He would no sooner get used to one den and make it his own but what they'd move him to another one.

The last one that contained him had no bars.

If he had been able to read his chart he would have known that he was considered on the way to recovery, that the authorities thought him almost "cured" of his aberration. The den with no bars was one that was used for limited liberty patients. They were on a kind of parole basis. But he had no idea of what the word meant and the first time he was released on his own cognizance, allowed to make a trip out into the "real" world, he put out of his mind the curious forms of "occupational therapy" with which the authorities were deviling him.

His daytime liberty was unreal and dragged by in a way that made him almost anxious to get back home to the new den.

He had all but made up his mind to do so, when the setting sun conjured up visions which he could not resist. In the dark he could get down on all fours!

Leaving the crowded city streets behind him he hurried out into the suburbs where the spring smells were making the night air exciting.

He had looked forward so to dropping on all fours and racing through the velvet spring night that when he did so, only to find that all the months of standing upright had made him too stiff to run, he could have howled. Then too the clumsy leather things on his back paws got in the way, and he would have ripped them off, but he remembered how soft his new pads were, and he was afraid of what would happen to them.

Forcing himself upright, keeping the curve in his back that he had found helped him to stand on his hind legs, he made his way cautiously along a flat thing that stretched off into the distance.

The four-wheeler that stopped near him would ordinarily have frightened him. But even his new weak nose could sniff through the rank acrid smells of the four-wheeler and find, under the too sweet something on the two-legged female, the real smell, so that when she said, "Hop in, I'll give you a lift," he did not run away. Instead he joined the she.

Her bark was nice, at first.

Later, while he was doing to her what her scent had told him she wanted done, her bark became shrill, and it hurt even his new dull ears. That, of course, did not stop him from doing what had to be done in the spring.

The sounds that still came from her got fainter as he

tried to run off on his hind legs. It was not much faster than a walk, but he had to get some of the good feeling of the air against his face, of his lungs panting; he had to run.

Regret was in him that he would not be able to get food for the she and be near her when she whelped, for that was the way of a wolf; but he knew too that he would always know her by her scent, and if possible when her time came he would be at her side.

Not even the spring running was as it should be, for without the excitement of being on all fours, without the nimbleness that had been his, he found that he stumbled too much, there was no thrill.

Besides, around him, the manifold smells told him that many of the two-leggeds were all jammed together. The odor was like a miasma and not even the all-pervading stench that came from the four-wheelers could drown it out.

Coming to a halt, he sat on his haunches, and for the first time he wondered if he were really, as he knew he was, a wolf, for a salty wetness was making itself felt at the corners of his eyes.

Wolves don't cry.

But if he were not a wolf, what then was he? What *were* all the memories that crowded his sick brain?

Tears or no, he knew that he was a wolf. And being a wolf, he must rid himself of this soft pelt, this hairlessness that made him sick at his stomach just to touch it with his two soft pads.

This was his dream, to become again as he had been. To be what was his only reality, a wolf, with a wolf's life and a wolf's loves.

That was his first venture into the reality of the world at large. His second day and night of "limited liberty" sent him hurrying back to his den. Nothing in his wolf life had prepared him for what he found in the midnight streets of the big city. For he found that bears were not the only males from whom the shes had to protect their young. . . .

And no animal of which he had ever heard could have moaned, as he heard a man moan, "If only pain didn't hurt

so much ..." And the strangled cries, the thrashing o
limbs, the violence, and the sound of a whip. He had neve
known that humans used whips on themselves too. . . .

The third time out, he tried to drug himself the way th
two-leggeds did by going to a big place where, on a screen
black and white shadows went through imitations of reality
He didn't go to a show that advertised it was in full gloriou
color, for he found the other shadows in neutral grays an
blacks and whites gave a picture of life the way his wolf eye
were used to looking at it.

It was in this big place where the shadows acted that h
found that perhaps he was not unique. His eyes glued to th
screen, he watched as a man slowly fell to all fours, threw
his head back, bayed at the moon, and then, right before ev
eryone, turned into a wolf!

A *werewolf*, the man was called in the shadow play. An
if there were werewolves, he thought, as he sat frozen in th
middle of all the seated two-leggeds, then of course ther
must be *weremen* (would that be the word?) . . . and he wa
one of them . . .

On the screen the melodrama came to its quick, bloody
foreordained end and the werewolf died when shot by a sil
ver bullet . . . He saw the fur disappear from the skin, an
the paws change into hands and feet.

All he had to do, he thought as he left the theatre, hi
mind full of his dream, was to find out how to become a
wolf again, without dying. Meanwhile, on every trip ou
without fail he went to the zoo. The keepers had become
used to seeing him. They no longer objected when he threw
little bits of meat into the cage to his pups. At first his she
had snarled when he came near the bars, but after a while
although still puzzled, and even though she flattened her
ears and sniffed constantly at him, she seemed to become re
signed to having him stand as near the cage as he possibly
could.

His pups were coming along nicely, almost full-grown
He was sorry, in a way, that they had to come to wolfhoo
behind bars, for now they'd never know the thrill of th

spring running, but it was good to know they were safe, and had full bellies, and a den to call their own.

It was when his cubs were almost ready to leave their mother that he found the two-leggeds had a place of books. It was called a *library*, and he had been sent there by the woman in the hospital who was teaching him and some of the other aphasics how to read and write and speak.

Remembering the shadow play about the werewolf, he forced his puzzled eyes to read all that he could find on the baffling subject of lycanthropy.

In every time, in every clime, he found that there were references to two-leggeds who had become four-leggeds, wolves, tigers, panthers . . . but never a reference to an animal that had become a two-legged.

In the course of his reading he found directions whereby a two-legged could change himself. They were complicated and meaningless to him. They involved curious things like a belt made of human skin, with a certain odd number of nail heads arranged in a quaint pattern on the body of the belt. The buckle had to be made under peculiar circumstances, and there were many chants that had to be sung.

It was essential, he read in the crabbed old books, that the two-legged desirous of making the change go to a place where two roads intersected at a specific angle. Then, standing at the intersection, chanting the peculiar words, feeling the human skin belt, the two-legged was told to divest himself of all clothing, and then to relieve his bladder.

Only then, the old books said, could the change take place.

He found that his heart was beating madly when he finished the last of the old books.

For if a two-legged could become a four-legged, surely . . .

After due thought, which was painful, he decided that a human skin belt would be wrong for him. The man in the fur store looked at him oddly when he asked for a length of wolf fur long and narrow, capable of being made into a belt . . .

But he got the fur, and he made the pattern of nail heads, and he did the things the books had described.

It was lucky, he thought as he stood in the deserted zoo, that not far from the cages he had found two roads that cut into each other in just the manner that the books said they should.

Standing where they crossed, his clothes piled on the grass nearby, the belt around his narrow waist, his fingers caressing its fur, his human throat chanting the meaningless words, he found that standing naked was a cold business, and that it was easy to void his bladder as the books had said he must.

Then it was all over.

He had done everything just as he should.

At first nothing happened, and the cold white moon looked down at him, and fear rode up and down his spine that he would be seen by one of the two-leggeds who always wore blue clothes, and he would be taken and put back into that other zoo that was not a zoo even thought it had bars on the windows.

But then an aching began in his erect back, and he fell to all fours, and the agony began, and the pain blinded him to everything, to all the strange functional changes that were going on, and it was a long, long time before he dared open his eyes.

Even before he opened them, he could sense that it had happened, for crisp and clear through the night wind he could smell as he knew he should be able to smell. The odors came and they told him old stories.

Getting up on all fours, paying no attention to the clothes that now smelled foully of the two-leggeds, he began to run. His strong claws scrabbled at the cement and he hurried to the grass and it was wonderful and exciting to feel the good feel of the growing things under his pads. Throwing his long head back he closed his eyes and from deep deep inside he sang a song to the wolves' god, the moon.

His baying excited the animals in the cages near him, and they began to roar, and scream, and those sounds were good too.

Running through the night, aimlessly, but running, feeling the ground beneath his paws was good ... so good ...

And then through the sounds, through all the baying and roaring and screaming from the animals, he heard his she's voice, and he forgot about freedom and the night wind and the cool white moon, and he ran back to the cage where she was.

The zoo attendants were just as baffled when they found the wolf curled up outside the cage near the feeding trough as they had been when they had found the man in the wolf's cage.

The two-legged who was his keeper recognized him and he was allowed to go back into his cage and then the ecstasy, the spring-and-fall-time ecstasy of being with his she ...

Slowly, as he became used to his wolfhood again, he forgot about the life outside the cage, and soon it was all a matter that only arose in troubled dreams. And even then his she was there to nuzzle him and wake him if the nightmares got too bad.

Only once after the first few days did any waking memory of his two-legged life return, and that was when a two-legged she passed by his cage pushing a small four-wheeler in front of her.

Her scent was familiar.

So too was the scent of the two-legged cub.

Darting to the front of his cage, he sniffed long and hard.

And for just a moment the woman who was pushing the perambulator that contained her bastard looked deep into his yellow eyes and she knew, as he did, who and what he was.

And the very, very last thought he had about the matter was one of infinite pity for his poor cub, who some white moonlit night was going to drop down on all fours and become furred ... and go prowling through the dark—in search of what, he would never know. . . .

# The Chessplayers

## by Charles L. Harness

Now please understand this. I'm not saying that all chess-players are lunatics. But I do claim that chronic chessplaying affects a man.

Let me tell you about the K Street Chess Club, of which I was once treasurer.

Our membership roll claimed a senator, the leader of a large labor union, the president of the A. & W. Railroad, and a few other big shots. But it seemed the more important they were *outside*, the rottener they were as chessplayers.

The senator and the rail magnate didn't know the Ruy Lopez from the Queen's Gambit, so of course they could only play the other fish, or hang around wistfully watching the game of the Class A players and wishing that they, too, amounted to something.

The club's champion was Bobby Baker, a little boy in the fourth grade at the Pestalozzi-Borstal Boarding School. Several of his end game compositions had been published in

*Chess Review* and *Shakhmatny Russkji Zhurnal* before he could talk plainly.

Our second best was Pete Summers, a clerk for the A. & W. Railroad. He was the author of two very famous chess books. One book proved that white can always win, and the other proved that black can always draw. As you might suspect, the gap separating him from the president of his railroad was abysmal indeed.

The show position was held by Jim Bradley, a chronic idler whose dues were paid by his wife. The club's admiration for him was profound.

But experts don't make a club. You have to have some guiding spirit, a fairly good player, with a knack for organization and a true knowledge of values.

Such a gem we had in our secretary, Nottingham Jones.

It was really my interest in Nottingham that led me to join the K Street Chess Club. I wanted to see if he was an exception, or whether they were all alike.

After I tell you about their encounter with Zeno, you can judge for yourself.

In his unreal life Nottingham Jones was a statistician in a government bureau. He worked at a desk in a big room with many other desks, including mine, and he performed his duties blankly and without conscious effort. Many an afternoon, after the quitting bell had rung and I had strolled over to discuss club finances with him, he would be astonished to discover that he had already come to work and had turned out a creditable stack of forms.

I suppose that it was during these hours of his quasi-existence that the invisible Nottingham conceived those numerous events that had made him famous as a chess club emcee throughout the United States.

For it was Nottingham who organized the famous American-Soviet cable matches (in which the U.S. team had been so soundly trounced), refereed numerous U.S. match championships, and launched a dozen brilliant but impecunious foreign chess masters on exhibition tours in a hundred chess clubs from New York to Los Angeles.

But the achievements of which he was proudest were his bishop–knight tournaments.

Now the bishop is supposed to be slightly stronger than the knight, and this evaluation has become so ingrained in chess thinking today that no player will voluntarily exchange a bishop for an enemy knight. He may squander his life's savings on a phony stock, talk back to traffic cops, and forget his wedding anniversary, but never, never, *never* will he exchange a bishop for a knight.

Nottingham suspected this fixation to be ill-founded; he had the idea that the knight was just as strong as the bishop, and to prove his point he held numerous intramural tournaments in the K Street Club, in which one player used six pawns and a bishop against the six pawns and a knight of his opponent.

Jones never did make up his mind as to whether the bishop was stronger than the knight, but at the end of a couple of years he did know that the K Street Club had more bishop-knight experts than any other club in the United States.

And it then occurred to him that American chess had a beautiful means of redeeming itself from its resounding defeat at the hands of the Russian cable team.

He sent his challenge to Stalin himself—the K Street Chess Club versus All the Russians—a dozen boards of bishop-knight games, to be played by cable.

The Soviet Recreation Bureau sent the customary six curt rejections and then promptly accepted.

And this leads us back to one afternoon at 5 o'clock when Nottingham Jones looked up from his desk and seemed startled to find me standing there.

"Don't get up yet," I said. "This is something you ought to take sitting down."

He stared at me owlishly. "Is the year's rent due again so soon?"

"Next week. This is something else."

"Oh?"

"A professor friend of mine," I said, "who lives in the

garret over my apartment, wants to play the whole club at one sitting—a simultaneous exhibition."

"A simul, eh? Pretty good, is he?"

"It isn't exactly the professor who wants to play. It's really a friend of his."

"Is *he* good?"

"The professor says so. But that isn't exactly the point. To make it short, the professor, Dr. Schmidt, owns a pet rat. He wants the rat to play." I added: "And for the usual simul fee. The professor needs money. In fact, if he doesn't get a steady job pretty soon he may be deported."

Nottingham looked dubious. "I don't see how we can help him. Did you say *rat*?"

"I did."

"A chessplaying rat? A four-legged one?"

"Right. Quite a drawing card for the club, eh?"

Nottingham shrugged his shoulders. "We learn something every day. Will you believe it, I never heard they cared for the game. Women don't. However, I once read about an educated horse . . . I suppose he's well known in Europe?"

"Very likely," I said. "The professor specializes in comparative psychology."

Nottingham shook his head impatiently. "I don't mean the professor. I'm talking about the rat. What's his name, anyway?"

"Zeno."

"Never heard of him. What's his tournament score?"

"I don't think he ever played in any tournaments. The professor taught him the game in a concentration camp. How good he is I don't know, except that he can give the professor rook odds."

Nottingham smiled pityingly. "I can give you rook odds, but I'm not good enough to throw a simul."

A great light burst over me. "Hey, wait a minute. You're completely overlooking the fantastic fact that Zeno is a—"

"The only pertinent question," interrupted Nottingham, "is whether he's really in the *master* class. We've got half a dozen players in the club who can throw an 'inside' simul for free, but when we hire an outsider and charge the members a dollar each to play him, he's got to be good enough to tackle *our* best. And when the whole club's in training for the bishop-knight cable match with the Russians next month, I can't have them relaxing over a mediocre simul."

"But you're missing the whole point—"

"—which is, this Zeno needs money and you want me to throw a simul to help him. But I just can't do it. I have a duty to the members to maintain a high standard."

"But Zeno is a rat. He learned to play chess in a concentration camp. He—"

"That doesn't necessarily make him a good player."

It was all cockeyed. My voice trailed off. "Well, somehow it seemed like a good idea."

Nottingham saw that he had let me down too hard. "If you want to, you might arrange a game between Zeno and one of our top players—say, Jim Bradley. He has lots of time. If Jim says Zeno is good enough for a simul, we'll give him a simul."

So I invited Jim Bradley and the professor, including Zeno, to my apartment the next evening.

I had seen Zeno before, but that was when I thought he was just an ordinary pet rat. Viewed as a chessmaster he seemed to be a completely different creature. Both Jim and I studied him closely when the professor pulled him out of his coat pocket and placed him on the chess table.

You could tell, just by looking at the little animal, from the way his beady black eyes shone and the alert way he carried his head, that here was a super-rat, an Einstein among rodents.

"Chust let him get his bearings," said the professor, as he fixed a little piece of cheeese to Bradley's king with a thumbtack. "And don't worry, he will make a good showing."

Zeno pitter-pattered around the board, sniffed with a

bored delicacy at both his and Bradley's chess pieces, twitched his nose at Bradley's cheese-crowned king, and gave the impression that the only reason he didn't yawn was that he was too well bred. He returned to his side of the board and waited for Bradley to move.

Jim blinked, shook himself, and finally pushed his queen pawn two squares.

Zeno minced out, picked up his own queen pawn between his teeth, and moved it forward two squares. Then Jim moved out his queen bishop pawn, and the game was under way, a conventional Queen's Gambit Declined.

I got the professor off in a corner. "How did you teach him to play? You never did tell me."

"Was easy. Tied each chessman in succession to body and let Zeno run simple maze on the chessboard composed of moves of chessman, until reached king and got piece of bread stuck on crown. Next, ve—one moment, please."

We both looked at the board. Zeno had knocked over Jim's king and was tapping with his dainty forefoot in front of the fallen monarch.

Jim was counting the taps with silent lips. "He's announcing a mate in thirteen. And he's right."

Zeno was already nibbling at the little piece of cheese fixed to Jim's king.

When I reported the result to Nottingham the next day, he agreed to hold a simultaneous exhibition for Zeno. Since Zeno was an unknown, with no reputation and no drawing power, Jones naturally didn't notify the local papers, but merely sent post cards to the club members.

On the night of the simul, Nottingham set up 25 chess tables in an approximate circle around the club room. Here and there the professor pushed the tables a little closer together so that Zeno could jump easily from one to the other as he made his rounds. Then the professor made a circuit of all the tables and tacked a little piece of cheese to each king.

After that he mopped at his face, stepped outside the circle, and Zeno started his rounds.

And then we hit a snag.

A slow gray man emerged from a little group of spectators and approached the professor.

"Dr. Hans Schmidt?" he asked.

"Ya," said the professor, a little nervously. "I mean, yes
sir."

The gray man pulled out his pocketbook and flashed
something at the professor. "Immigration Service. Do you
have in your possession a renewed immigration visa?"

The professor wet his lips and shook his head wordless-
ly.

The other continued. "According to our records you
don't have a job, haven't paid your rent for a month, and
your credit has run out at the local delicatessen. I'm afraid
I'll have to ask you to come along with me."

"You mean—*deportation?*"

"How do I know? Maybe, maybe not."

The professor looked as though a steam roller had just
passed over him. "So it comes," he whispered. "I know I
should not haf come out from hiding, but one needs money...."

"Too bad," said the immigration man. "Of course, if
you could post a $500 bond as surety for your self-support—"

"Had I $500, would I be behind at the delicatessen?"

"No, I guess not. That your hat and coat?"

The professor started sadly toward the coat racks.

I grabbed at his sleeve.

"Now hold on," I said hurriedly. "Look, mister, in two
hours Dr. Schmidt will have a contract for a 52-week exhibition tour." I exclaimed to the professor: "Zeno will make
you all the money you can spend! When the simul is over tonight, Nottingham Jones will recommend you to every
chess club in the United States, Canada, and Mexico. Think
of it! Zeno! History's only chess-playing rat!"

"Not so fast," said Nottingham, who had just walked
up. "I've got to see how good this Zeno is before I back
him."

"Don't worry," I said. "Why, the bare fact that he's a
rat—"

The gray man interrupted. "You mean you want me to wait a couple of hours until we see whether the professor is going to get some sort of a contract?"

"That's right," I said eagerly. "After Zeno shows what he can do, the professor gets a chess exhibition tour."

The gray man was studying Zeno with distant distaste. "Well, okay. I'll wait."

The professor heaved a gigantic sigh and trotted off to watch his protégé.

"Say," said the gray man to me, "you people ought to keep a cat in this place. I was sure I saw a rat running around over there."

"That's Zeno," I said. "He's playing chess."

"Don't get sarcastic, Jack. I was just offering a suggestion." He wandered off to keep an eye on the professor.

The evening wore on, and the professor used up all his handkerchiefs and borrowed one of mine. But I couldn't see what he was worried about, because it was clear that Zeno was a marvel, right up there in the ranks of Lasker, Alekhine, and Botvinnik.

In every game, he entered into an orgy of complications. One by one his opponents teetered off the razor's edge, and had to resign. One by one the tables emptied, and the losers gathered around those who were still struggling. The clusters around Bobby Baker, Pete Summers, and Jim Bradley grew minute by minute.

But at the end of the second hour, when only the three club champions were still battling, I noticed that Zeno was slowing down.

"What's wrong, professor?" I whispered anxiously.

He groaned. "For supper he chenerally gets only two little pieces cheese."

And so far tonight Zeno had eaten twenty-three! He was so fat he could hardly waddle.

I groaned too, and thought of tiny stomach pumps.

We watched tensely as Zeno pulled himself slowly from Jim Bradley's board over to Pete Summers'. It seemed to take him an extraordinarily long time to analyze the position on Pete's board. At last he made his move and crawled across to Bobby Baker's table.

And it was there, chin resting on the pedestal of his king rook, that he collapsed into gentle rodent slumber.

The professor let out an almost inaudible but heart-rending moan.

"Don't just stand there!" I cried. "Wake him up!"

The professor prodded the little animal gingerly with his forefinger. "*Liebchen*," he pleaded, "*wach auf!*"

But Zeno just rolled comfortably over on his back.

A deathly silence had fallen over the room, and it was on account of this that we heard what we heard.

Zeno began to snore.

Everybody seemed to be looking in other directions when the professor lifted the little animal up and dropped him tenderly into his wrinkled coat pocket.

The gray man was the first to speak. "Well, Dr. Schmidt? No contract?"

"Don't be silly," I declared. "Of course he gets a tour. Nottingham, how soon can you get letters off to the other clubs?"

"But I really can't recommend him," demurred Nottingham. "After all, he defaulted three out of 25 games. He's only a *Kleinmeister*—not the kind of material to make a simul circuit."

"What if he *didn't* finish three measly games? He's a good player, all the same. All you have to do is say the word and every club secretary in North America will make a date with him—at an entrance fee of $5 per player. He'll take the country by storm!"

"I'm sorry," Nottingham said to the professor. "I have a certain standard, and your boy just doesn't make the grade."

The professor sighed. "*Ja, ich versteh'.*"

"But this is crazy!" My voice sounded a little louder than I had intended. "You fellows don't agree with Nottingham, do you? How about you, Jim?"

Jim Bradley shrugged his shoulders. "Hard to say just how good Zeno is. It would take a week of close analysis to say definitely who has the upper hand in *my* game. He's a pawn down, but he has a wonderful position."

"But Jim," I protested. "That isn't the point at all. Can't you see it? Think of the publicity ... a chess-playing *rat* ...!"

"I wouldn't know about his personal life," said Jim curtly.

"Fellows!" I said desperately. "Is this the way all of you feel? Can't enough of us stick together to pass a club resolution recommending Zeno for a simul circuit? How about you, Bobby?"

Bobby looked uncomfortable. "I think the school station wagon is waiting for me. I guess I ought to be getting back."

"Coming, doc?" asked the gray man.

"Yes," replied Dr. Schmidt heavily. "Good evening, chentlemen."

I just stood there, stunned.

"Here's Zeno's income for the evening, professor," said Nottingham, pressing an envelope into his hand. "I'm afraid it won't help much, though, especially since I didn't feel justified in charging the customary dollar fee."

The professor nodded, and in numb silence I watched him accompany the immigration officer to the doorway.

The professor and I versus the chessplayers. We had thrown our Sunday punches, but we hadn't even scratched their gambit.

Just then Pete Summers called out, "Hey, Dr. Schmidt!" He held up a sheet of paper covered with chess diagrams. "This fell out of your pocket when you were standing here."

The professor said something apologetic to the gray man and came back. "*Danke,*" he said, reaching for the paper. "Is part of a manuscript."

"A *chess* manuscript, professor?" I was grasping at straws now. "Are you writing a chess book?"

"Ya, I guess."

"Well, well," said Pete Summers, who was studying the sheet carefully. "The bishop against the knight, eh?"

"Ya. Now if you excuse me—"

"The bishop versus the knight?" shrilled Bobby Baker, who had trotted back to the tables.

"The bishop and knight?" muttered Nottingham Jones. He demanded abruptly: "Have you studied the problem long, professor?"

"Many months. In camp . . . in attic. And now manuscript has reached 2,000 pages, and we look for publisher."

"*We. . . ?*" My voice may have trembled a little, because both Nottingham and the professor turned and looked at me sharply. "Professor"—my words spilled out in a rush—"did Zeno write that book?"

"Who else?" answered the professor in wonder.

"I don't see how he could hold a pen," said Nottingham doubtfully.

"Not necessary," said the professor. "He made moves, and I wrote down." He added with wistful pride: "Zenchen is probably world's greatest living authority on bishop-knight."

The room was suddenly very still again. For an overlong moment the only sound was Zeno's muffled snoring spiraling up from the professor's pocket.

"Has he reached any conclusions?" breathed Nottingham.

The professor turned puzzled eyes to the intent faces about him. "Zeno believes conflict cannot be cheneralized. However, has discovered seventy-eight positions in which bishop superior to knight and twenty-four positions in which knight is better. Obviously, player mit bishop must try—"

"—for one of the winning bishop positions, of course, and ditto for the knight," finished Nottingham. "That's an extremely valuable manuscript."

All this time I had been getting my first free breath of the evening. It felt good. "It's too bad," I said casually, "that the professor can't stay here long enough for you sharks to study Zeno's book and pick up some pointers for the great bishop-knight cable match next month. It's too bad, too, that Zeno won't be here to take a board against the Russians. He'd give us a sure point on the score."

"Yeah," said Jim Bradley. "He would."

Nottingham shot a question at the professor. "Would Zeno be willing to rent the manuscript to us for a month?"

The professor was about to agree when I interrupted. "That would be rather difficult, Nottingham. Zeno doesn't know where he'll be at the end of the month. Furthermore, as treasurer for the club, let me inform you that after we pay the annual rent next week, the treasury will be as flat as a pancake."

Nottingham's face fell.

"Of course," I continued carefully, "if you were willing to underwrite a tour for Zeno, I imagine he'd be willing to lend it to you for nothing. And then the professor wouldn't have to be deported, and Zeno could stay and coach our team, as well as take a board in the cable match."

Neither the professor nor I breathed as we watched Nottingham struggling over that game of solitaire chess with his soul. But finally his owlish face gathered itself into an austere stubbornness. "I still can't recommend Zeno for a tour. I have my standards."

Several of the other players nodded gloomily.

"I'm scheduled to play against Kereslov," said Pete Summers, looking sadly at the sheet of manuscript. "But I agree with you, Nottingham."

I knew about Kereslov. The Moscow Club had been holding intramural bishop-knight tournaments every week for the past six months, and Kereslov had won nearly all of them.

"And I have to play Botvinnik," said Jim Bradley. He added feebly, "But you're right, Nottingham. We can't ethically underwrite a tour for Zeno."

Botvinnik was merely chess champion of the world.

"What a shame," I said. "Professor, I'm afraid we'll

have to make a deal with the Soviet Recreation Bureau." It was just a sudden screwy inspiration. I still wonder whether I would have gone through with it if Nottingham hadn't said what he said next.

"Mister," he asked the immigration official, "you want $500 put up for Dr. Schmidt?"

"That's the customary bond."

Nottingham beamed at me. "We have more than that in the treasury, haven't we?"

"Sure. We have exactly $500.14, of which $500 is for rent. Don't look at me like that."

"The directors of this club," declared Nottingham sonorously, "hereby authorize you to draw a check for $500 payable to Dr. Schmidt."

"Are you cuckoo?" I yelped. "Where do you think I'm going to get another $500 for the rent? You lunatics will wind up playing your cable match in the middle of K Street!"

"This," said Nottingham coldly, "is the greatest work on chess since Murray's *History*. After we're through with it, I'm sure we can find a publisher for Zeno. Would you stand in the way of such a magnificent contribution to chess literature?"

Pete Summers chimed in accusingly. "Even if you can't be a friend to Zeno, you could at least think about the good of the club and of American chess. You're taking a very funny attitude about this."

"But of course you aren't a real chessplayer," said Bobby Baker sympathetically. "We never had a treasurer who was."

Nottingham sighed. "I guess it's about time to elect another treasurer."

"All right," I said bleakly. "I'm just wondering what I'm going to tell the landlord next week. He isn't a chessplayer either." I told the gray man, "Come over here to the desk, and I'll make out a check."

He frowned. "A check? From a bunch of chessplayers? Not on your life! Let's go, professor."

Just then a remarkable thing happened. One of our most minor members spoke up.

"I'm Senator Brown, one of Mr. Jones's fellow chessplayers. I'll endorse that check, if you like."

And then there was a popping noise and a button flew by my ear. I turned quickly to see a vast blast of smoke terminated by three perfect smoke rings. Our rail magnate tapped at his cigar. "I'm Johnson, of the A. & W. *We chessplayers* stick together on these matters. I'll endorse that check, too. And Nottingham, don't worry about the rent. The senator and I will take care of that."

I stifled an indignant gasp. I was the one worrying about the rent, not Nottingham. But of course I was beneath their notice. I wasn't a *chessplayer*.

The gray man shrugged his shoulders. "Okay, I'll take the bond and recommend an indefinite renewal."

Five minutes later I was standing outside the building gulping in the fresh cold air when the immigration officer walked past me toward his car.

"Good night," I said.

He ducked a little, then looked up. When he answered, he seemed to be talking more to himself than to me. "It was the funniest thing. You got the impression there was a little rat running around on those boards and moving the pieces with his teeth. But of course rats don't play chess. Just human beings." He peered at me through the dusk, as though trying to get things in focus. "There wasn't really a rat playing chess in there, was there?"

"No," I said. "There wasn't any rat in there. And no human beings, either. Just chessplayers."

# Mop-Up

## by Arthur Porges

When he had quartered the stricken land in vain for almost two years without finding another living person, the man came upon a witch, a vampire, and a ghoul holding solemn parley by a gutted church.

As he broke through the tangled, untrimmed hedges into the weed-grown garden, the witch laughed shrilly; and as if mocking her own white hairs, danced widdershins, cackling in delight. "There's one left, just as I thought, and a very pretty fellow, too!" She was a revolting old beldame, and he stared at her aghast.

The vampire, lean and elegant in a rusty black cloak, arose with his ruby eyes kindling. He crouched a little and a pointed tongue flickered between full, soft lips. Catlike, he glided forward.

"Stop!" the witch cried. "He's the last, fool! Would you drink him dry? You must learn to use the blood of beasts.

Remember, Baron—there's probably not another human in the whole world."

The vampire showed his enormous canines in a sly smile.

"You underestimate me, Mother. All I had in mind was a mere sip. It's been two years, and there's nothing quite like the fresh stuff, so strong and warm."

"No!" she protested. "He's mine. Not a drop. The poor darling's worn enough. There are plenty of animals left to suck on."

"Not for me—yet," was the lofty retort. "I prefer the blood banks. They'll keep me supplied for many years. People collected millions of pints, all nicely preserved, carefully stored, rich and tasty—then never got to use them. What a pity! Still," he added, his voice wistful, "cold blood is hardly the drink for a nobleman of my lineage."

"Blood banks!" she chortled, displaying strong, discolored teeth. "So that's where you've been getting it all this time. I wondered." She nodded cynical approval. "Then there's no problem, because *his* kind"—with a contemptuous gesture towards the ghoul huddled beastlike behind them—"are set for ages, too. Nothing to do but pick and choose." Her stringy jaw muscles knotted. "So the man is mine!"

The ghoul gave him a single wicked glance, and continued digging at his clogged incisors with fingernails like splinters of glass. The man's stomach heaved; he gulped down a sour taste.

"Don't be afraid, darling boy," the hag crooned. "You're safe with us. And it's worth a deal to be snug these days, I can tell you."

He stood there, haggard and feverish, thinking himself mad. Among the survivors, if any, he had expected the usual proportion of carrion crows, but nothing like this fantastic trio. Still, perhaps, even their company was better than the wrenching ache of complete isolation in a ravaged world. Two of them, at least, were outwardly human.

"You're not crazy," the witch reassured him, pinching his stubbled cheek. "You'll live long and well to serve me."

She eyed him with a kind of leering coyness, utterly grotesque in an ugly old woman. "A fine, strong fellow. What a sweet lover he'll be for poor Mother Digby. I'll teach you the 435 ways—"

"Am I the last?" he muttered. "Really the last? I've searched. I—"

"Yes," the vampire said, with a melancholy smile. "Unfortunately, I fear you are." The ghoul tittered, and his eyes filmed over like oily, stagnant pools.

"Don't frighten him," she flared. "Sit down my honey. Here by me." She pulled him to her side, and dazed, he submitted.

"Tell me the truth," he begged again. "Am I actually the only one left?"

"Yes. First came the hydrogen bombs. It was something to see. I've been around a long time, my lad: the big Mississippi Quakes in 1815, Krakatoa, Hiroshima—they were nothing by comparison. The Baron knew it was coming— how did you know, hey? He won't tell." She snapped her fingers and laughed jeeringly; her bony elbow prodded the man. "Ah, it was the blood banks! I might have guessed— right?"

The Baron nodded coolly. "Yes. When they began to pyramid the stock piles, I suspected what would happen soon. That's when I told you to look out for fire. One atomic blast would have burnt your juiceless carcass to cinders." His lips twitched at her outraged expression. "As a nobleman, I was almost tempted to warn the most ancient monarchies of Europe. For the upstart Americans, with their absurd 'democracy,' I care nothing. Rule by comic book! But in the Balkans—" He broke off with a sigh.

"Germs, Mother," the ghoul croaked suddenly, giving her a doglike glance of worship.

"Right, my pet. The germs came next. Every country had secret cultures, deadly soups of plagues old and new. How the people died! All but my lovely man here." She patted his thigh. "Why are you still alive, hey?"

He shook his head. "There was a new, untested serum

in our lab—a last attempt. Just a tiny drop. I had nothing to lose." He brooded a moment in silence, then asked, "How about Europe—Asia?"

"Wiped out. Nobody left. Not one saucy little Mamselle, or golden Eurasian, or cool English girl for you. Take old Mother Digby, and be satisfied. Don't let my wrinkled face fool you! Wine long in the cask is best!"

He shuddered away from her. "How can you be sure? About Europe?"

"There are ways. Before we lost contact with our fellows, I received regular reports; and since then I've made many flights on my own. Paris, London, Belgrade, Copenhagen—it's all the same. Some by bombs; more by disease."

"Where are Ours—the Others?" the ghoul demanded in a thick voice.

"Who knows?" she snapped, her lips tightening. "At the last Sabbath, few came. Maybe the old customs are dying as the silly humans died. Anyway, I've seen none for weeks now. Neither has the Baron." She turned back to the pale, bemused man. "Did you find any of your kind?"

"No," he admitted dully. "Only animals, and always huddled in groups. As if *they* were appalled, too. But—you're certain about the other countries?"

She flourished a veiny hand. "Clean sweep. From Tibet to Los Angeles. We cover oceans in hours, the Baron and I. *He*," sneering at the ghoul, "can only snuff about the ground." The ghoul winced. "You're the last human, all right. I knew one was about somewhere. I can tell. But no more rosy throats for the Baron, even if "—with a malicious smile—"he didn't prefer the easier method with blood banks!"

"Not much choice," was the unashamed reply. "And besides, people were getting harder to manage in these days of—ah—enlightenment. Even *he* was faced with a new problem: cremation."

A bubbling snarl came from the crouched ghoul.

"Never mind," the witch soothed him. "Your troubles have been over, these two years. No more cremation again, ever."

"We've just had cremation wholesale," the vampire pointed out. "And speaking of troubles," he jibed, "yours are not over, dear Mother. No orgies, no backsliding church folk to torment, who's to care now if you dry up a cow?"

She ignored him, snuggling closer to the man. "Adam and Eve," she simpered, resting her white head on his shoulder.

"Don't!" He shrank away.

She glared at him. "Will you, will you," she hissed. "Don't cross me, my puling innocent, or—!"

"He's good for only a short time at best," the vampire reminded her, pleasantly solicitous. "After that—"

"You lie!" she screeched. "By my arts he'll live a thousand—ten thousand—years. He'll learn to love me. And if you dare to touch him!"

The Baron shrugged. He winked at the man. "Ignore her threats to you. You're so valuable to the lecherous old hag that she wouldn't harm—what's that?" He rose to his full height, pointing.

Far out in the brush, a faint, bobbing light twinkled, then another.

"Fireflies," the witch said, indifferently. She stroked man's hand, and tried to press her leather cheek to his.

"No," said the ghoul. Doglike, he sniffed the air, his damp snout quivering.

A moment later, two rabbits hopped into the garden. One of them cautiously drew nearer. It stopped about ten feet away, and rose up on his hind paws, with ears up. Its button of a nose twitched. They watched the animal in amazement.

"They're certainly tame around here," the man muttered. He sensed a possible diversion, and alerted himself for escape. But he felt little hope. How could a lone mortal elude this dreadful trio?

The rabbit squeaked loudly, peremptorily, and a larger animal came up behind it, laboriously hauling in its jaws something that trailed on the ground.

"That's a beaver," said the man, unobtrusively edging away.

As the animal approached, they recognized its burden: a freshly felled sapling, one end gnawed to a rough point.

Suddenly the rabbit uttered a series of high, chirping sounds, strangely modulated. It waved one snowy paw in a gesture of command. The beaver responded with an irritable grunt, wrestling its clumsy stick forward. The dancing lights reappeared, very close now: tiny, flaming torches, gripped in the handlike paws of two raccoons, each running jerkily on three legs.

The rabbit made a new, imperious motion; it pointed directly at the squat, silent ghoul.

The witch broke into a laugh, and startled, the rabbit crouched, poised for flight. "Animals!" she jeered. "Attacking *us*!" She turned to the grave Baron. "You heard that rabbit—it's actually giving some sort of orders." She pointed a derisive finger at the rodent, small and wary, studying her with soft, luminous eyes. "Hey, there—do you think we're afraid of beavers and such vermin?"

"Wait." The vampire clutched her arm. "I doubt if they understand English. It's some simple language of their own. They've learned a lot in two years—if the whole thing didn't really begin much earlier. Mother, this is a serious matter. Don't you see? The stake's for me; the fire is for you; and for *him*, I imagine—"

The ghoul gave a hollow, moaning cry, and dived crashing into the nearest bushes. A moment after, there was a thin, bestial howl of pain. Then the underbush crackled, and the ghoul stumbled back into the garden. He lurched blindly towards the witch, and they saw that his face was gone, leaving something like a wet sponge, soft and amorphous. The man stared in frozen horror, oblivious of his opportunity. There was a deep-chested growl from the weeds, and a great, shaggy form shambled out. It was a grizzly bear, grim and implacable, with bloody foam on its champing jaws.

Gasping, the witch leaped aside. The mangled ghoul groped for her, whimpering in fear. Silently the bear padded forward, its heavy coat rippling. But before it could close in, there was a quavering shriek like a woman in torment, a tawny blur, and a mountain lion, sickle claws wide spread, landed squarely upon the ghoul's back, smashing him to the ground.

Screaming hoarsely, the blinded monster writhed, clutching with thick, earth-stained fingers for his assailant. But the lion's hind legs were already gathered for the disembowelling stroke, and the ghoul had no chance. It was soon over; the quasi-human body lay still. The panther sat back, licking its great paws like any kitchen tabby. It paused once to give the man a sidelong, inscrutable glance. His pulse leaped to a new realization. Was the lion promising deliverance?

"Mother," the vampire said composedly, "this is the finish. Now we know where the Others went." There was a tinge of weariness in his accented voice. "Well, a nobleman does not fear—death." He pronounced the last word almost wonderingly.

"Idiot!" snarled the witch. "We're not earthbound like that—" thrusting a finger at the torn ghoul.

The Baron gave a fatalistic shrug, met her challenging gaze, and smiled. He pulled his cloak tight, dislimned, and began to shrink. When he seemed about to vanish completely, there was a smoky flash, and a huge bat winged up from the garden, a spectral silhouette against the sunset sky. The black cloak lay empty on the grass.

A sonorous belling rang in the distance, harsh, yet mournfully musical, the call of a moose. Even in the circumstances, the man thrilled to the heady sound, recalling past hunts. The rabbit squealed in excitement, pointing upward. And they came, almost in military formation: a vast flight of birds, all predators of the air. Eagles, falcons, and hundreds of smaller piratical hawks, swift and rakish. They swooped with raucous cries; the sky throbbed to their wingbeats. A mighty golden eagle led the attack, hurtling 2,000 feet straight down, to strike with open talons. They heard the wind whistling through its stiff feathers and the crisp impact as the half-mile swoop reached a climax in that shattering blow.

The bat crumpled, disrupted in mid-air. It spun downward, erratic as a falling leaf, and there, in the weedy garden, the vampire reappeared, broken-backed.

As he squirmed, trying desperately to arise, the beaver drew near with its crudely-pointed sapling. Just out of reach, it paused, earnest and phlegmatic, its whiskered face indicating a solemn concern with the task ahead. The vampire glowered with concentrated malignance as a host of smaller animals pattered up. Sharp teeth and tenacious claws pinned the writhing thing, while four chipmunks held the stick upright in their facile paws, the point upon the heaving breast.

Then, from the darkening thicket, a bull moose emerged. He moved with stately tread, his split hooves clacking. On reaching the thrashing vampire, he snorted once, as if in profound distaste, and stood there waiting. The rabbit snapped its paw down in a vertical arc, and with a single blow of his massive forefoot, the moose drove the stake home.

Squawking imprecations, the witch abandoned her vain aerial search for an opening in the umbrella of birds, dropped heavily a dozen feet to the earth, and with ragged white locks streaming, crashed through the ranks of lesser animals. One of them grated in agony. But the witch halted abruptly, cowering. She looked about with darting, baleful eyes, a hunched figure of evil. They poured into the garden from all sides: bears, panthers, badgers, and two purebred bulls, wickedly horned and bellicose. Overhead, the hawks circled, watching with fierce yellow eyes. The man saw the beasts converge, backing her steadily toward the church wall, a fire-scarred, crazily tilted brick barrier. There were muffled sounds, and he heard clearly a wheezy sobbing. He smiled briefly, and some of the tension left him. The raccoons, like conspirators in their dark masks, raced in with torches, followed by dozens of beasts, dragging twigs and bark. An old, gaunt cow ambled by with a fence rail in her worn jaws. She peeped at the man with liquidly compassionate eyes. Before long, the pyre flamed high against the blackened wall. There was a final wailing cry as the witch died.

He dropped to his knees emotionally exhausted. They had freed him. The beasts of the forest and farm: the burly, comical black bears, the sullen, feral grizzlies, the pretty rabbits and squirrels, even an old cow, doubtless filled with affection for some mouldering barnyard where children had laughed and people had once been kind. All these had joined to deliver the last man.

Touched, he peered through the growing dusk at the rabbit, trying to convey his gratitude and delight. There would be a new Golden Age, wherein man and beast might live in loving harmony. He forced back guilty visions of timid deer horribly wounded, of dying birds cheerfully ravaged by his dog. But that was past. No more hunting for him. Instead, he would teach them man's wonders. He would—

The rabbit hopped aside, and four lean wolves pressed forward, licking black lips. A bull pawed the earth, bellowing. High above, an early owl hooted.

The rabbit faced the wolves, pointing to the man with one paw, the other poised in a familiar manner.

The man understood that pregnant signal, and the soft, purring sounds he had begun to make died in his throat. It was thumbs down.